# A Year in Ink

## Volume 18

# A YEAR
## in ink
### San Diego Writers, Ink Anthology Volume 18

Edited by W.A. Fulkerson and Vera Sanchez

THE
INK SPOT
PRESS

*A Year in Ink, Volume 18* is a publication of
The Ink Spot Press
San Diego Writers, Ink
ARTS DISTRICT Liberty Station
2730 Historic Decatur Road
Barracks 16, Suite 204
San Diego, CA 92106

Many thanks go to our authors, editors, first readers, Arin Winkler,
Laurie Gibson, Madi Bucci, Kristen Fogle, Emily Greenberg, Niayla Brazil,
The Mingei International Museum, and everyone else who contributed to
this work.

Prose edits by Laurie Gibson

Cover and layout design by Arin Winkler

Cover image by Leslie Pierce
www.artistlesliepiercestudio.com

ISBN: 978-0-9998925-8-9
Printed in the United States of America
Printed by IngramSpark

# Contents

# A YEAR in ink

San Diego Writers, Ink
Anthology Volume 18

# Prose

Writing is such a paradox.

On the one hand, it takes tremendous courage to put your heart on display, to be vulnerable enough to infuse your works with the real you so that what you write can impact someone else. Writing authentically (the only form of writing worth reading) means that the writer has to look at the hard things in life, examine their flaws, their traumas, their sins, their fears, and their failures. Aren't there sweet and wonderful parts of life as well? Of course there are, and authentic writing must have these also, but the darkness provides the depth, the shading, the contours.

It takes courage to look at those things, to rob the grave of its treasures and yet have strength enough to return to the realm of light.

On the other hand, writing is a compulsion—something you *have* to do. This is hard to explain to someone who has never felt the need to "sit down at a typewriter and bleed," as Hemingway said. The ancient Greeks said, "Sing in me, Muse," as if there were something beyond themselves giving them the words, ushering them forward, and they were almost helpless to tell the tales that came to their lips unbidden.

It is a fearful thing to speak, yet speak we must. It is a burden and a gift, a blessing and a curse, a pleasure and a pain, a foolishness and a wisdom all wrapped up in one.

In brief, it is a manifestation of being human—something good that is inextricably cracked, yet beautiful, whole, full of potential and paradox.

This year's authors dared to set out on this well-worn road, yet in a way that no one else has done before. You will see themes of aging and acceptance, of fear overcome, of sweet moments, the winking eye, love found, and love lost. We honor them here for their courage, but we also read to discover what the "muses" wrote—to observe the miracle of spinning stories to see what timeless truths and experiences they illuminate.

I invite you now to sit down, sift through these pages, and participate in the wonderful paradox of prose.

—W.A. Fulkerson
Prose Editor, *A Year In Ink, Volume 18*

# Taking the Leap

## Adhara Mereles

Lucia took three steps back, ran to the edge of the cliff, and jumped off. At last, she permitted herself to lose control. To let herself fall. To embrace fear, and find a certain freedom in those lasting seconds.

Just thirty minutes prior, she'd been tearing her hair out at home. Trying to shake off her writer's block. Consumed by pressure. Pressure to produce, to succeed, to be good enough. Her short story— stuck beneath the weight of composition, lost in the depths of unresolved structure.

*That's it.* Lucia slipped on her black bikini, lathered her skin with sunscreen, threw on her rainbow-colored "Ask Me About My Pronouns" baseball cap, and sauntered to the coast. The balmy seventy-seven-degree day wrapped her in warmth. She kicked her writer's block to the shore and breathed in the salty air. At the end of her street, a horseshoe-shaped cove spread its glistening waters to the horizon.

Lucia descended the concrete stairs, slipped off her flip-flops, and relaxed into the softness of the earth. Finding her place along the shore, she laid out her white towel and stretched out. Bundles of beachgoers dappled the scene. A mash-up of conversation, reggae music, and seagull yelps echoed along the landscape.

In the distance, Lucia observed a group of boys perched over the towering cliff as they studied the tides. When a wave arrived, one of them took a running start and leaped into the sea. Her stomach dropped as the boy flew through the air. To her relief, he hit the ocean with a tremendous splash, came up for air, and egged the rest of his friends on. The sight awoke a thirst for adventure inside her.

Lucia took a deep breath, lumbered up the cliff, and waited her turn. The distance from the top to the surface below tickled her tummy with intimidation. But she exhaled and blew her nerves into the wind. Determined to take the leap.

"Don't do it." A familiar, authoritative voice pierced the space behind her.

She turned around to face her nemesis, Control, his skin matted like a mangy coyote.

"Control, get outta here." Lucia shooed him away.

A wave rolled in, catching the corner of her eye. That's when Lucia ran to the edge of the cliff and jumped. In those moments, she welcomed it all. The fear-based butterflies flew from her core until she couldn't sense them anymore. The pressure to succeed vanished into the scent of seaweed. All the contest and submission deadlines she'd been stressing over dissolved into the future. She gave into the present—the exquisite unknown, the delicious mystery of falling, and trusted her trajectory.

Her body plummeted into the ocean with a refreshing splash. Submerging her "I," she lost all concept of herself, her ego, and her expectations.

When she surfaced, she noticed Control poised inside a rustic boat, holding a fishing pole.

"What kind of no good are you up to now?" Lucia smacked the water's surface.

"I'm fishing for syntax." Control pulled at the rod, checking for tension. "By golly. There's a whole school of it down below, along with commas, structure, dialogue, sensory details, emotionality, character development, and themes. You hear me, Lucia, I'm gonna prepare a literary feast for you tonight so you can finish that story you've been working on."

"Ew, no. Fuck that shit, I'm taking time to play."

Eager to ditch Control, Lucia dove under the boat and flipped it upside down. Unable to swim, Control sank into the abyss with an alarming "Nooooo!"

With Control out of the picture, Lucia stopped swimming and paused. Time slowed. She slowed. She stopped rushing. She stretched out her limbs and floated face up like a sea star, surrendering to the swells. She observed the pelicans soar overhead. She let the ocean lift her up, take her down—fling her body all around. She relished the sensation of the sand swooshing between her toes. She witnessed a patina of foam hover over the water's surface. She gasped at the waterfalls that formed along the faces of large rocks when the waves drenched them. She listened to the sizzling sound of the surf kissing the shore as whitecaps danced beneath the sun.

And when she got home that evening, she infused her story with a plethora of new connections. Her connection to nature, to her community, to herself. Her story's creative message of inspiration bloomed so powerfully that it lifted itself off the page—sailing into the night sky. Embellished with love. Its sweetness reached hearts around the globe, weaving a contagious, connective thread between them—saturated with possibility.

# Sunshine and Rainbows

## Bernie Nofel

When we got off the train, it was raining. And I mean it was coming down. This was no delicate drizzle leaving minute drops, like fairies' kisses, on our cheeks and foreheads. It wasn't a whimsical spring sprinkling. A misty, gentle, moistening. A dewy dampening. A lighthearted watery caress.

No, this rain was punitive. Scolding. Like the principal's paddle. In a Catholic school. This rain came down in bludgeoning blows, angry, malicious, malevolent, watery explosive weapons striking with ill intent. These were the minions, the billions of children borne of clouds that woke up on the wrong side of bed and couldn't find a dog to kick.

It wasn't raining cats and dogs. It was raining lions, and tigers, and bears.

Oh my.

We got off our train into this tortuous torrent, slapped in the face by the blinding monsoon, immediately burdened and beaten down into a sidewalk-facing crouch, fighting forward in tiny steps against a wicked witch's whirlwind, and stood out in that dismal drench waiting for a cab.

Of course, we didn't have raincoats or umbrellas. We could have had raincoats and umbrellas. We didn't have raincoats or umbrellas.

Why, you ask?

Because some genius, some cocksure crank, some Bizarroland reverse King Solomon, some buffoon filled with nearly as much bluster as the hurricane we were stuck in, said the following: "Oh, it's not going to rain today. Trust me. I know."

My name's Joe, and I'm that errant weather prognosticator. Those words belonged to me. Which made the storm not just painful, but bitter. On me, it was raining last night's coffee, soaked in sauerkraut.

That was the first day of our trip.

I expected, no I predicted, it would only go downhill from there.

"Honey," my wife, Matilda, shouted, barely audible about the dowsing din. "Honey, do you think it's going to stop raining soon?"

Now, a better man would have learned. Accepted his limitations. Grown from his earlier mistake. Maybe considered that weather forecasting might not be his strength. Perhaps, some suggestion of fallibility, some tenuous response lacking certitude might inform his upcoming prediction.

A better man might appreciate that a meaningful response would benefit from things he currently lacked. Like knowledge. And facts.

Yes, I believe—no I know—that that's exactly what a better man would do.

Instead, I looked up from the sidewalk, allowing the balloons of sauerkraut coffee to burst and fill my eyes and accost my face. I squinted into the face of that scowling sky threatening to pick us up and tornado us to Oz. I turned to look in one direction, then the next. I scratched my head, rubbed my chin, pulled at my left ear and then my nose.

"Matilda," I said as confidently as a man counting how many fingers he had while looking at his own hand. "Matilda, I guarantee you that it's going to completely stop raining in fifteen minutes."

A lesser woman would have rolled her eyes. Considered and accepted the truth about her flawed husband's unreliable declarations. Guffawed and harumphed. Questioned my character. Lost faith in my good judgment. Instead, Matilda gave me a big hug, anticipating the predicted, imminent clearing of the sky, exactly as I'd prophesied.

Then we stood there, in the rain, under an unrelenting tumultuous tempest that hadn't abated the slightest bit when a cab finally rescued us forty-five minutes later.

We flopped exhaustedly into the back seat like drowning pirates plucked from a maelstrom. The cab driver asked, "You folks think it'll stop raining soon?"

I winced in anticipation of some scathing mention of my flawed weather forecasting. Cowered toward the door in expectation of some well-deserved disparaging comment. Flinched and shrank waiting for the verbal tempest, born of my own foolhardiness, to be unleashed.

Instead, without hesitation Matilda answered, "I have it on good authority it's about to completely stop raining any moment."

We looked at each other, and shared a sunbeam smile. A smile of blue skies in our hearts.

We bundled together closer and tighter on the way to the hotel, and stared peacefully out windows blurred from the unabated waterfalls flowing down the glass.

Hand in hand.

Wet arm in wet arm.

Floating on rainbows every rainy mile of the way.

Together.

# The Stingaree

## Marie Lagos

When the pianist concluded his play, the blindfolded incumbent began to play the same piece, and within the first few stanzas, had completely shattered any hope for the challenger. The crowd went crazy as the reigning dueling-piano-champion's fingers fluttered across the keys as effortlessly and elegantly as a hummingbird's wings. He was playing the same song as the challenger, but he'd embellished the melody, making it even more amazing than the first version.

"He's extraordinary!" I noted to Gerard, who was slipping an arm around the back of my chair. I moved away. He didn't seem to notice, for he was speculating with James Reid and John Banks about how much money Mr. Davenport must be pulling in from this show, and whether they should consider opening such a bar in Illinois, and how Gerard should be the one to do it.

When the song ended, the crowd leapt from their seats and pounded out emphatic applause in favor of the incumbent. Mr. Davenport made his way toward the dueling pianos, hoisted the incumbent from the bench, and turned him toward the crowd.

I stared at the pianist and furrowed my brow, cocking my head this way and that, for even blindfolded, he looked oddly familiar. Yet, that was impossible, as I knew no one in town.

"Ladies and gentlemen!" Mr. Davenport announced. "Once again, your winner!"

And then it dawned on me. "Is that...."

"David Romero!" the proprietor shouted.

My mouth fell open as I gaped at David, hand held up by Mr. Davenport as the victor of the duel.

"Now, my fine audience!" Mr. Davenport continued. "We will require another challenger. Who here is up for the task?" As he scanned the crowd, a young man with a heavy mustache came forward, took a seat at the piano, and began to plunk out a worthy rendition of a lively piece. But the moment his fingers sunk into the keys, I knew he was doomed. I smiled, silently rooting for David. The challenger finished his efforts, and David took on the same song, masterfully improving it tenfold. I wondered then, whether he had even played the song before, or whether he had heard it for the first time, right then and there, and repeated what he could remember and made up the rest, improvising and enhancing as he went along. Either way, he was a master at the piano, and it was no contest. The crowd demanded he again be declared the winner, and the challenger slumped away, retreating to his friends to be consoled with drink.

"Dare I ask for another?" Mr. Davenport said, searching the crowd for a volunteer. But it seemed David had scared the hell out of anyone else who might have considered taking him on. "Anyone? Anyone?"

"You do it," Gerard nudged me.

I laughed at the absurdity.

"You said you play. Challenge him."

"Absolutely not!"

"Why not?" Rebecca joined in. "He's been challenged by all these silly men, and I haven't seen a single lady take him on."

"Because I'm not a silly lady," I said. "He's really good. And I haven't played in a very long time. I could never take him on and face myself the next day." Or face *him* the next day.

"Do it!" Connie said.

"Enough!" Gerard threw up his hands to calm the pack. "Enough already! The lady says she doesn't want to. She won't agree to it so...." He grabbed my hand and yanked me up from the table. "I'll agree for her. Ed! Over here! We have a challenger!"

I glared at Gerard, who was grinning like a madman, while the rest of my table goaded him on. As Mr. Davenport made his way toward us, Gerard planted his lips on mine. I pulled away, cringing at the stench of whiskey on his breath. I was furious for so many reasons, and my heart was pounding like a war drum. I had a mind to curse him out, but the annoying voice of Annabelle St. James echoed in my ears. He had paid for a parlor girl, and I had to play the part. I took a deep breath to try to calm my nerves and my temper. And it must have been the need to get away from Gerard that allowed Mr. Davenport to lead me toward the piano.

"Ladies and gentlemen! Our first lady challenger of the night!"

The crowd went wild, and I looked around, my cheeks flushing hot-red with self-consciousness. I had only ever played at church, and with my piano students in San José, and that one time in Los Angeles with Gauthier Lenoir. But I was not a performer. I was a quiet lover of music, and in no way was I an entertainer.

I turned back to Mr. Davenport. "Do you have sheet music?"

"Right there." He pointed to a tin bucket stuffed with worn-out manuscripts, frayed and overused, torn and withered at their edges. I looked back at David, who was seated on the other side of me, blindfolded and patient. He wore a bit of a smirk, which was enough to ignite the spark of competition in me, and I decided then that I would very much like to beat him. I sifted through the pages and found nothing that looked remotely interesting or complex enough to surpass him. And then, my fingers grazed words I recognized.

I slipped the sheet of Joplin's "Maple Leaf Rag" onto the music rack and sat down, scooting the bench closer to the piano so I could reach the pedals. I laced my fingers together and stretched out my arms and drew in a deep breath.

"Whenever you're ready, miss," Mr. Davenport said.

Someone whistled, and I glared in their general direction.

"Go easy on her, David!" someone shouted.

I started in on the beginning chords of the song and wasn't even ten seconds in when David stood up. I stopped. Mr. Davenport rushed to him. "What's a matter, son?"

"With all due respect to Scott Joplin," David said, "I'm *not* playing 'Maple Leaf Rag' for the tenth time tonight. For land's sake, isn't there another song these people who call themselves musicians know? Never mind." He started to pull off his blindfold. "I've already proven I'm the best, and surely *no woman* would prove differently."

The crowd cheered. Men banged glass pints against wooden tables, and even the women in the room betrayed me with their cackles and hoots. Mr. Davenport grabbed David's hands to stop him from removing the blindfold, just as I shot up from the bench.

"First of all!" I shouted over the rumble, and the mass began to quiet down. "I *would* prove differently." I leered at David even though he couldn't see me. "But if you are too chickenhearted to discover that for yourself, Mr. Romero, then forfeit!" The crowd roared and stomped their feet in excitement. David turned his head in my direction, and I noticed—but only because I was transfixed on him—the corner of his mouth turned up, ever so slightly, and I wondered whether he recognized my voice. No matter; the rush of competition had bolstered me. "And secondly and most importantly, *I will make your fingers bleed!*"

The smirk on David's face, along with the madness of the crowd, were enough. And I knew what I had to do. I sat back down and flung the Joplin manuscript back into the bucket to the bellows and howls of the audience. Mr. Davenport guided a blindfolded David back down to his bench. I took a deep breath, touched my fingers to the keys, and pounded out as quickly and accurately as I could, the most complex sound I knew and one I was certain David didn't: the ferociously passionate Third Movement of Beethoven's "Moonlight Sonata." It was normally a long piece, a good six minutes or so, but I shortened my play to only a few minutes so David wouldn't have enough time to figure out the chords. And when I was finished, the audience burst from their chairs, clapping and cheering and hooting even more loudly than they'd done for David before. Rebecca was applauding so vigorously I thought her hands might dislocate from her wrists. Mr. Davenport hurried to me, lowered onto one knee, and kissed my hand.

"Will you marry me?" he asked, and I burst into laughter. Even David, who was still seated at his piano, was chuckling. The proprietor turned to him. "Alright, son, if you dare."

David grinned as he stretched out his fingers. He sank them into the keys and played nearly flawlessly the exposition of Beethoven's Third Movement—blindfolded. I thought he must have lied to me before about not knowing the piece, which would have been rather fortuitous given the circumstances under which we'd discussed it. He made it nearly a half-minute in without a slip, but then he began to struggle, made up a few lines—which no one else would have noticed—but couldn't get himself back on track and finally pressed his fingers into the keyboard, pounding out a dull E chord, and stopped.

The crowd was silent, waiting for him to try it again. David threw his hands up in defeat and shook his head.

The audience exploded, leaping to their feet, hammering out a furious applause, some of them calling out jeers to David for suffering defeat to a woman. Mr. Davenport rushed over to me and lifted my hand in the air.

"Our winner!" he shouted. "What's your name, darlin'?" I glanced at David before responding, and Mr. Davenport repeated, "Lorelei Flores!" David jerked his head in my direction, and I felt a twinge of smug satisfaction at having whipped him. He ripped off the blindfold and stared at me, his eyes fixed on mine. A smile slowly overtook his mouth, and he knelt down, pretending to grovel at my feet. I laughed at the exaggerated gesture of defeat.

He rose, then said, "You're amazing, *Sirenita*. You'll do the world injustice if you stop playing."

The crowd continued to roar around us. He lifted my hand to his lips and drew me into him, grasping the small of my back so we were touching at the waist. I drew in a sharp breath at the bold move.

"And you look stunning," he murmured into my ear. His hot breath made me tingle. "Although I do prefer to see you in your nightdress in my saloon."

# You Asked for It, Honey

## Anne Randerson

If we're lucky, the voices of our loved ones remain with us our entire lives. I'm nearly sixty, but I still remember most things my maternal grandmother taught me. Grams wasn't a typical grandma; she couldn't bake or sew. Yet she was an athlete, an artist, a healer, and a Scorpio—like me. She even water-skied on her head.

Grams was fifty-three years older than me, and my hero.

Every August, for two whole weeks, I got to hang out with her at the beach. Those sunny San Diego summers were my best childhood memories. Each morning, I'd wake up to rustling pages and her scratchy pen. I'd prop my head on my elbow and—as sunlight poured through the curtains, gracing her arthritic knuckles—watch her fill her "dream diary." I couldn't wait for her to finish and reveal her nocturnal adventures. To pass the time, I'd scrutinize her oil paintings over our twin beds, searching for hidden messages in her bold, impressionistic strokes.

Grams would scribble on. At last, she'd sigh and set down her pen. "Read it, Grams," I'd plead.

She'd nod and—in her hoarse morning voice—recite her latest dream. As a psychotherapist, she liked to refer to Freud and Jung, sparing no details, not even to a kid. In her analysis, she didn't just rely on their interpretations; she'd add plenty of her own ideas, and—I liked to think—some of mine.

One memorable morning, when I was thirteen, Grams taught me a lesson I'd never forget.

She donned her pink jogging suit and headed for the shore. At the water's edge, she stood still as a mountain and shut her eyes. Waves crashed around us; seagulls flew overhead. Salt crusted the air; sand covered our toes. Time stopped. At last, when my patience nearly ran out, Grams inhaled deeply and began her morning tai chi.

I stood a few paces behind her shadow, attempting to imitate her slow, graceful movements. Joggers whizzed past; couples with toddlers and dogs paused to stare. But Grams was too focused on her moves to notice—and I was too busy trying to copy her.

Grams' routine always took a half hour, but I gave up after three minutes. My limbs got sore, suspended in the air, and I cringed when kids my age rolled their eyes at us. So, I plopped in the sand and watched Grams swirl in slow motion, like waves dancing in the sea.

My favorite part came at the end. Ever so slowly, she spread her arms and lifted her right knee into the air. Then, in one swift movement, she cocked her right foot, extended her leg, kicked an imaginary opponent, and retracted her foot, which gently landed. Then, she continued with her routine. Until that fateful morning when I got impatient and blurted out, "Can't you go any faster?"

Grams squinted at me. "Of course I can, honey," she replied, lowering her heel. "But that's not the point. Tai chi is all about controlling your movements, relaxing your body and mind, allowing vital life energy to flow through your system to create health and harmony." She pointed at the crashing waves. "It's also about nature." She glanced at her wrinkled toes nestled in the sand. "And blending into your surroundings."

I must have seemed disappointed, so she continued: "But to answer your question, of course I can go faster. Tai chi is still a martial art. In fact, it's the basis of kung fu."

*Yeah, right.* Grams was solid enough, but in her pink outfit, cotton-ball hair, and crinkly skin, she was no Jackie Chan. At least, not to me.

"No way, Grams. Are you trying to tell me this is like kung fu?"

Grams' lips cracked into a smile. "You bet it is."

I giggled. "Prove it to me then."

Her blue eyes sparkled. "Fine. Get behind me."

I did what she asked, unconvinced. *This is silly.*

"Now, attack me from the back."

*No way.* I shook my head. "Come on, Grams. I'm not about to attack—"

Just then, my brothers showed up. After all, it's not every day your grandma demonstrates her kung fu moves on your sister.

"Are you chicken or what?" she countered. She might have looked like Grams, but she sure didn't sound like her.

"Okay, if that's really what you want." My cheeks grew hot. "Ready?" I asked, backing up while holding my breath.

Grams shot back: "Ready as ever. Go for it!"

I clenched my teeth. *You asked for it....* With all my might, I flung myself at my grandmother, my arms locking around her chest. Then, sneaky as a snake, Grams crossed her arms, slid them under mine, and inserted her right foot behind my ankle.

"Hayaaa!" she yelled, flinging her arms open and extending her right leg.

Arms flailing, I flew backward, landing with an ungracious thud in the sand.

My brothers cheered as I bit the dust. "Do it again, Grams!"

No way. I'd had enough. Luckily, we were on the beach; otherwise, I might have broken my back.

What did Grams do next? Eyes twinkling, she gazed down at me and whispered, "You asked for it, honey."

# A Lesson in Tobacco

## M. Annette Ketner

We followed our Granddad down the lane to the barn, my six-year-old brother Buz and me, little nuisance helpers ready to pet the cows while Granddad milked them.   He placed the three-legged stool at just the right angle and got to work. The barn cats knew the pattern and gathered around waiting for the stream of milk to hit their open mouths.

When the cows were milked and the pails of milk dumped into the separator, Granddad took out a paper envelope with chewing tobacco in it, broke off a chunk, and put it in his mouth.

"Can I have some, too?" Buz asked.

"My chewin' tobacco?"

"Yes, please."

"You sure about that? You want to learn to chew and spit?" My granddad confirmed the request.

"Yes. It looks like fun." Buz was right—my granddad was an expert at hitting the spittoon from any number of different angles and distances. It was truly quite remarkable. And the bump in his right cheek made him look like some kind of lumpy warrior.

Granddad thought a few minutes and then said, "Sure. You can have a chew. But you have to let me know if you like it." With that, my granddad tore off a piece of chewing tobacco and handed it to Buz.

"What about you, Sis, you want to try it, too?"

Well, that's where my better sense left me. True, I was eighteen months younger than Buz, but I usually had better judgement, even then. But under the pressure of the moment, I caved.

"Yes, I do." Part of that response was curiosity. Part was envy. But the biggest part was that I didn't want my brother to get ahead of me in these important life experiences.

So, chew we did.

The taste was really bad, kind of a cross between biting into an onion and a rotten egg. The chunk and the saliva it generated filled my mouth and I didn't have much room left to ask any questions.

So, not only did we chew. But we swallowed.

A small detail Granddad forgot to mention. You're not supposed to swallow chewing tobacco. Who knew? I mean, we had watched him put a plug in his mouth and everything else that goes in your mouth gets chewed and swallowed, right?

Within a short time, my stomach began to rumble. As the minutes went on, it rumbled louder and louder until I had to run to the outhouse with the intention of throwing up there.

I did not make it that far.

Close behind me came Buz, also on the same mission. He did make it to the outhouse, ran right past me, down on the ground on all fours in great distress.

All of a sudden, my grandma appeared looking quite upset. She wiped my face with the wet dish cloth she had in her hand and went on to rescue Buz from the outhouse.

"You kids head for the kitchen. I'll help you get that awful taste out of your mouth and find something to settle your stomach."

We hurried into the house, but Grandma stopped. She wasn't done with Granddad yet.

"Dad, what were you thinking? Giving these kids chewing tobacco and making them sick? You coulda killed them. What do you have to say for yourself?"

He looked up with a twinkle in his eye and answered triumphantly, "You can bet-cher-boots neither one of them will ever try tobacco again!"

And he was right.

We neither smoked nor chewed nor sniffed—ever.

Granddad lessons might be tough, but, by gosh, they are effective. And like Granddad said, some last a whole lifetime.

# Stephen Returns

## Donna Jones

Chartres, France
August 1083

A clatter in the courtyard announced the men's return. The messenger sent ahead to share the news of Stephen's victory. His impending arrival had given them some time to prepare, but they had thought they would have at least one more day, and all was not yet ready. Adela was not ready.

As soon as she heard the drumbeat of so many horses trotting over the drawbridge, Adela's insides clenched, as if her stomach were forming itself into a fist, preparing to defend an expected attack. She granted herself a moment to steady her thoughts. Focused on her belly, she willed it to release its knots. To no avail. *Oh well, it was worth a try*, she thought, before bracing herself to greet the husband she had not seen for months.

It had been a relief, his absence. The formal politeness in every interaction between them since their wedding night had both depressed and, over time, enraged her. None of this was her fault. And nothing she tried had helped the situation—the most irritating thing of all. With him off fighting, she had been bored and lonely, but at least she had enjoyed not having the daily reminder that her husband did not want her. And now, too soon, her respite was ending.

Would he even come to greet her, or would he focus his attention on his father and stepmother, as they eagerly awaited him? It would be embarrassing if, amidst the many couples embracing, her husband greeted her with only a stiff bow or nod of the head. But she could expect no better, given the state of their relationship before he departed. Worse, he might act even more resentful than he had before, blaming her for the news of Emma's marriage and subsequent move to England. Did he even know about Emma? He must. Emma surely had written him of her plans. But what if she had not? Was Adela to be the one to inform him? No, a wife was not responsible for reporting on the whereabouts of her husband's mistress. No doubt the news would soon reach him, now that he was home.

Adela's footsteps slowed as the colors of a castle full of those who had been left behind all those months ago swirled around her, the herbs sprinkled in the rushes yesterday releasing their sweet scent into the air with each step. The noise was deafening, as hundreds of exhausted, exhilarated men made their way into the Great Hall, crashing into their loved ones rushing to greet them. The servants were almost tripping one another as one group arranged the tables for the forthcoming meal, another carried in buckets of water for the baths required to wash weeks of dust off the highest-ranking men, and still another gathered supplies to treat the wounded. The most heartbreaking those whose unfortunate duty was to prepare for burial the dead arriving by cart. The fresh minty smell was already dissipating, overpowered by the other, ranker, more familiar scents of men and blood and sweat.

"Pardon, milady," her newest maid said after accidentally bumping Adela while snaking her way through the crowded hall to locate a certain young squire. The two had just begun courting when the king demanded Stephen lay siege to an overly ambitious lord Philip had decided was a threat, or, more likely, had treasure Philip felt would better serve himself. The girl had been moping around the castle ever since the men had left, leaving no doubt of her feelings toward the young squire who had been finding excuses to be around her before duty had called.

"It's fine, Helene, no harm done. Now go, welcome home your Simon." Her maid was blushing now, both with embarrassment at having bumped her mistress and excitement at seeing the boy she had been missing, as well as surprise her mistress knew his name. She stood still, unsure of what to do.

"Go on," Adela repeated, as her maid curtseyed and hurried out, her head turning as she struggled to locate the face which, despite its pox scars, held Helene's dreams. Tears came unbidden to Adela's own eyes, then, to her embarrassment, and she quickly wiped them off and blinked rapidly to stop any further flow. After experiencing for herself the troubles that love caused in her own family, she had solemnly vowed to protect her heart at all costs. Despite that, some part of her craved having someone to love, and to love her. Some place deep inside wanted to feel what Helene felt, no matter the pain and heartache it would undoubtedly bring.

She thought then of the man who had created such fire within her that it had almost made her forget her vow. The man who had rescued her from almost certain death from the tusks of a hungry boar, on that day that already seemed a lifetime ago. She closed her eyes, remembering, thinking of the lushness of his lips as he had asked if she was injured, the feeling that the roughness of his callused hands had sent up and down her body as he checked her for broken bones before lifting her gently so she could sit up, with care unexpected in a battle-hardened knight. No. Adela shook her head, clearing her mind of such thoughts. She must not dwell on him. Especially now, at this moment, when the man to whom she had sworn her loyalty was here, undoubtedly expecting a gracious welcome from her.

If her mother taught her anything, it was the vital importance of appearances. She had grown up knowing that she was always being watched and must never forget to arrange herself to create the image that best suited her purpose. Perception was as important as reality and would get you far. That was her mother's teaching, though so far following it had gotten her only here, to this place of her misery. She must nonetheless somehow make the best of her circumstances. That required at least seeming excited to greet her husband. Adela forced herself to arrange her face as if she were excited for her husband's safe and victorious return.

And Stephen's mission had been a success. He had rid the king of an unruly vassal and had thus created a debt Philip now owed them. A debt they could store away for use later, when the need arose. As it surely would. At least, Adela was grateful for that. Focusing on an unattainable man would not benefit anyone, especially her.

She straightened up, forcing her shoulders back and her head high, glancing around the bustling hall, and forcing her mouth upward into the best semblance of a smile. But she could feel her lips quivering. That would not do. She tried again. She thought of how it would feel if it were her childhood friend Laethard arriving to visit. There. That was better. Now her smile held steady, and it almost matched her eyes.

"My lord," Adela said, dropping into a curtsy as she saw her husband make his way into the hall before she could reach the courtyard. Stephen paused, said something to the man beside him, then walked toward her, with strides that seemed somehow more confident than she remembered from before.

"My lady."

Then, before she knew what was happening, her husband—the one who had barely looked her in the eyes in the months since their wedding—took her hand, lifted it, and pressed his lips against her skin. Before she could process what that could mean, he bent down and kissed her on the mouth. Briefly, barely touching, and so quick that she could almost wonder if it really happened. But a kiss, nonetheless. Adela's eyes widened, and she cocked her head, ready to say something, anything, to break the awkwardness that washed over her with this unexpected display of intimacy when she sensed her father-in-law staring at them. She glanced over at Thibaut and nodded her head at him to acknowledge she had seen his need.

"It appears your father is eager to hear from you."

"Indeed," Stephen answered, turning toward the proud old man. "Duty calls. I look forward to hearing about all I missed, and telling you about my own adventures, over dinner."

"Yes, of course," Adela said, hoping her voice did not shake, and sensing the heat flush her face at this unexpected greeting. With that, Stephen squeezed her hand gently, in some unspoken communication that held a promise within it. He trailed his thumb ever so lightly along the top of her hand as he finally, reluctantly, released it, and she felt herself shiver.

"It's cold in here," she said, hugging herself then, embarrassed.

"Go, warm up," Stephen said, broadly smiling with what seemed genuine happiness. His eyes—bluer than she had realized, as if the sky itself had filled them—smiled at her in a way that matched the upward curve of his mouth. Then he left to regale his father with the details of the battle, the number of men lost, what spoils from victory they had won, and to learn what his father expected of him next. Adela stood rooted to the spot for a moment, for fear that if she moved too quickly, her legs may fail her. She allowed herself a moment to observe her husband as he greeted the count and realized she was fixating on his hands. The ones that had just held hers. That somehow were still generating heat in the center of her own hand, in the place his lips had touched.

What did it mean? Had he missed her? All questions without answers, that she must ponder until Thibaut first learned all he needed to know from his son. Her stomach spoke again, this time with excitement. Enough of such nonsense. There was work to be done. Adelaide must accept her offer of help this afternoon, given that ensuring a proper celebratory welcome for the knights was more important than a petty exercise of power and control. At least Adela could hope. She needed something to keep herself busy, to settle her stomach and her thoughts.

# A Mother and Her Faith

## Alejandra Navarro

Three days a week, a family member walked Flora Martinez to mass at St. Joseph's Church.

Her family, especially her adult children, believed Flora—the five-foot, two-inch woman who home-birthed six children, including one large-headed, ten-pound boy; the woman who migrated 1,980 miles from Guanajuato to California over an unforgiving land and into an uncertain future with a stranger who later became her husband; the woman who negotiated and collected wages for her family's work in the walnut orchards; the woman who hoisted on her back the guilt of losing her first son when she was sixteen—was incapable of walking four blocks alone.

As the Martinez family matriarch, Flora spoke few words and emoted even less. She smiled so infrequently that friends must have thought she had to pay for each show of teeth. And yet, she had the tranquil disposition of someone who didn't worry. Her expression was permanently neutral, and her voice always calm. Worry, fear, and agitation coursed through her veins but remained tucked under her long, floral cotton dresses. Instead, these feelings emerged in the form of deep creases on her forehead and around her small oval eyes and ravaged her once-beautiful mahogany locks into thin wisps of graying hair she coiled at the nape of her neck.

Flora caught a glimpse of her reflection in the window of a flower shop a block away from the church. Her hair appeared whiter than the salt-and-pepper she was used to seeing.

"Mama, let me color your hair," her daughter Rosanna pleaded one morning last week. "It will look so good! You shouldn't have to be gray!"

"You're going to leave me with half a head of white hair when it grows out," Flora chided in Spanish, waving off the idea. "No!"

"I'll keep coloring your hair," Rosanna said, pulling at one of the strands that never seemed to grow long enough to reach her mother's bun. To make her mother laugh, the girl added, "And if I don't, you'll just look like the neighborhood *bruja*! A witch casting your spells." Rosanna rubbed her hands together and gave her an evil grin before releasing a loud cackle.

Flora let her lips curl up into the start of a smile, which she knew would make Rosanna happy.

Rosanna responded by puckering her painted-red lips and blowing her mother a kiss. With big eyes, long eyelashes, and a shapely body, her daughter often caught the spotlight and the attention of most men. Flora worried about Rosanna more than her other children. She was not clever enough to sneak out of the house at night unseen, but smart enough to make her boyfriend a fiancé. The thin engagement band on Rosanna's finger comforted Flora. The official wedding date was nine weeks away. The thought of what could happen in nine weeks whittled a deeper crease along her brow and gave her another reason to attend church.

Her youngest daughter, Loli, pulled her from her thoughts when she took her mother's arm.

"We're going to be late," said Loli, who was delivering her mother to church this morning. Flora smiled at the daughter whose decisions never whittled creases into her aging, fragile skin.

Life had weathered Flora to appear older than her forty-seven years. But Flora was not weak or easily intimidated. While her family feared for her safety when she walked down the crumbling street to the church, Flora did not.

In her home, Flora was the authority. She commanded and received respect. Often, one raised eyebrow was enough to strike fear into her children, even as they grew into adulthood. She only had to use the back of her hand once—two or three times with the hard-headed boys—to show she was in charge.

Flora never understood that her children didn't fear her strikes or the wrath of Satan she promised would fall upon them if they misbehaved. Her children feared disappointing her. They each wanted her affection, which made them obedient.

Her eldest son, Jose, would have joined the priesthood, the ultimate blessing for Flora, had he not fallen in love with a girl who was now the mother of his children.

Loli was the youngest child, at sixteen, but the most responsible. She questioned the church too much to be devout in her faith, but she had strong morals. Of all her children, Flora expected Loli to stay on a good path. Loli was the daughter who would get married and stay married; the daughter who would raise a nice, large family; the daughter who would take care of her parents when they were old— a time Flora could feel approaching faster than she'd like.

"It's my duty to put my children on the right path, or get them as close to it as I can," Flora had shared with Father Jim when he stopped by her house for coffee.

He paused and gave her a sympathetic smile before he responded, "We do what we can."

On this Sunday, Loli and Flora arrived fifteen minutes early for the eight o'clock mass at St. Joseph's. They dipped their fingers in the holy water at the front door and made the sign of the cross. Not stopping to chitchat with neighbors congregating for gossip, Flora led the way to the east side of the church reserved for lighting candles and saying prayers, especially for those most in need of God's grace. She lit two candles at every mass she attended.

"Who are these candles for, Mamá?" probed Loli, finally working up the courage to ask. "You always light two. That's not enough for everyone in the family."

"One is for the family," Flora replied.

"Who is the other one for?" The curious girl was relentless. "Why do they need this? And, does it really make a difference to light a candle for someone?"

Flora took her daughter's hand, patted it, and then spent one of her smiles. The unusual sight of her mother's happiness distracted the girl, and the questions melted from her thoughts like wax flowing down the side of a prayer candle. Flora placed her coins in the donation collection box and left to find her seat. Speechless, her daughter followed.

Flora sat in a pew near a stained-glass window with the image of the Virgin Mary holding baby Jesus. Draped in a royal blue cloak, Mary gazed at a pink baby Jesus with the rays of a rising sun behind them. The vivid display of a mother's love gave Flora hope. "A mother cannot always protect her children from the dangers they face, but her eternal love will always be present to guide them," she whispered to herself.

Flora and Loli sat, stood, kneeled, and prayed. Flora kept one hand on a rosary in her dress pocket. Since this was the English mass, they recited English responses to the priest from memory.

"Praise to you Lord, Jesus Christ."

Flora did not get in line for communion. All of her living children had been baptized and had celebrated their First Holy Communion, Flora made sure of that, so they could walk to the altar to receive the Eucharist.

Flora could not get in line to receive the holy wafer because she had never had her First Holy Communion. Flora did not grow up Catholic or with religion of any kind; her own parents made sure of that. She found religion on her journey to the United States. She never knew she needed God until she found herself alone on a desert path, miles from any other living soul, holding her lifeless baby in her arms.

"Lord, hear our prayers," the crowd recited.

Her children tried to reason with her.

"No one would know if you took the holy wafer," her son Juan would tell her.

"God would know," Flora insisted.

But at the end of every mass, Flora casually slipped into the confessional.

None of her children asked why she would not take communion but would confess. Flora assumed that by the end of the mass they were too tired to untangle her reasoning. And for that, she was grateful. Confession was private, between her and the priest and God. Flora needed to confess. This God also knew.

Her children would wait for her in the same spot in the last pew. Once she had recited her Our Fathers and Hail Marys and asked for forgiveness, they would join her in the vestibule to dip a finger into the holy water once more and make a departing sign of the cross.

Flora was just about to head to a pew to say her penance when she noticed Loli was not there. She could not see the girl, which was unusual.

She headed toward the exit, and then spotted her daughter lighting a candle. From a distance, the girl looked like a woman standing tall in a fitted dress that highlighted the curves emerging from her once boyishly thin physique. Flora watched Loli look up at the painting of Jesus on the crucifix hanging above the prayer candles. Her hand rested on her tummy. Then Loli bowed her head in prayer before tapping her forehead, her heart, each shoulder, and then her lips.

Flora quickly retreated and stood by the confessional door when Loli came around a column. Her eyes were glossy.

"I wanted to look at the stained-glass pictures on that side of the church," Loli said, answering a question her mother had not asked.

Flora nodded and continued out of the church, not stopping to say her penance.

As they walked home, Flora felt an additional weight of something unspoken but very wrong. It was settling itself on her back beside the guilt she carried for her firstborn. Loli had set aside her questions and criticism of the church to light a candle, but for what exactly, Flora wondered. Questions fluttered in her mind. *To ask for guidance for what she should do? To ask for forgiveness for what she had done? To ask for peace for what was done to her?* Flora only knew that her daughter was asking for God's grace.

She gazed back at the church. Still in the shadow of its towering presence, she grasped the rosary in her pocket, felt the first bead, and began reciting the prayers.

Loli walked ahead of her, into the sunlight, and kept her eyes locked on the road ahead.

# Such a Silly Thing

## Aimee Truchan

I push the last meatball around my plate soaking up flakes of parmesan. Mom's full pile of spaghetti sits in front of her. You don't know a slow eater until you sit down with a woman who replaced a standard-sized utensil with a shrimp fork around the age of eighty. "Then I eat less," she says upon questioning. This is something that bothers Lisa but makes me smile. I wonder what eccentricities I will develop as I age. I wonder who might observe them, write about them, laugh.

I surrender to a second helping, mom's homemade meatballs so tasty and tender they can barely keep their shape from pot to plate. The red sauce is thick, tangy, and sweet, the result of an all-day simmer.

"I just don't know why she insists on going through with this silly thing."

"Mom, the divorce is happening. And, it's not a silly thing."

I don't know if all children from big families know what it feels like to be talked about behind their backs or just those from Italian Catholic ones. A parent diving deep into one child's life with a sibling, aunt, or cousin is as much tradition as is Sunday sauce.

"Well, I know. But why? What did he do wrong?"

"I don't think he did anything. It doesn't matter. It's none of our business."

"Dave is just such a nice man. They've been married twenty years."

"If she's not happy, Mom, isn't that twenty years too many?"

The sadness on Mom's face tells me she's jealous or at the very least, genuinely confused. Yes, Lisa married a very nice, soft-spoken man. A man who never challenged Lisa, never raised his voice nor his hands. A man polar opposite to the one our mother married—cold and unloving on a good day; hot-headed and violent on a bad one. How dare Lisa throw him away! How dare she not appreciate what she has!

I don't tell mom that Dave's calm, passive demeanor often equated to cowardice. That when Lisa needed him to stand up to a loud neighbor or address a rude waiter, he couldn't. That when their two sons needed discipline, Dave caved and catered to their every whim. That both Jason and Tyler were becoming bullies, trying to be the man their father wasn't. My mother would never swallow any of that.

"The thing is, Mom—Lisa is your child. Even if the divorce would be one hundred percent her fault, you're supposed to defend her, not him. Please, whatever you do, don't say these things to her."

"Oh no, I'm only telling you." Mom's famous line when she's gossiping.

"Okay, good."

My plate is becoming empty again. Mom sits quiet for a minute or two.

"I guess I just know what it feels like."

"What *what* feels like, Mom?"

"I know how it feels to try so hard to do everything right, to try to be perfect. To do everything to please someone and it's still never good enough."

Warm tears fill my eyes. What a fool I am. She misses him; she's not relieved he's gone the way that I am; the way I had always hoped she'd be. She didn't stay with him out of fear or obligation. She'd loved him.

I'd never considered such a silly thing.

# Rock Bottom Was Calling My Name

## Tammy Tollner

After surviving our first Covid Christmas, it dawned on me that I was absolutely exhausted. ALL THE TIME. Every. Single. Day.

Something about my drinking had changed. The buzz I got from a couple glasses of wine was short and the repercussions I felt the next day were so much worse. Every morning, until happy hour rolled around, I was in misery.

(But did I do Dry January? Heck no—that's for amateurs!)

I wanted to blame my exhaustion on the stress of living with Covid and the changes that it brought to our household. The uncertainty of lockdowns, schools closing, and our young adult "kids" moving back home. The bummer of postponing our wedding.

And of course, the actual virus that was lurking, skipping, and morphing around the globe. But in my gut I knew there was another reason I felt so terrible.

As the months of the pandemic dragged on and the news got scarier, wine o'clock at our house started earlier. More Pinot Grigio became my way to numb the stress of living in a world in panic mode and a home now bursting at the seams.

Every one of our six children came home to live with us during the pandemic at one time or another. The two youngest already had their own rooms, but the four oldest had been living on their own *for years*. There were breakups, roommate changes, leases ending, homes bought and sold. Two of those four brought their dogs.

We don't have a dog. There's a very good reason we don't have a dog.

WE HAVE RAISED SIX KIDS AND WE ARE TIRED!

Luckily, we loved their sweet and adorable pups, but it took a while to adjust to all the stuff that went with them. For example: slobbery windows and poo in unexpected places.

Our kitchen was ALWAYS open. Everyone ate at different times and there was a wide range of work, school, sleep, and lounging schedules.

Some cleaned up after themselves better than others. Many mornings I awoke to a sink full of dishes after a late night jacuzzi party and nosh fest—the plates, bowls, and wineglasses stacked, Tetris-style in the sink—*six inches* from the dishwasher.

Both sets of washing machines and dryers were continually spinning something or at the very least, full of someone's damp and forgotten load of sports bras, leggings and thirty-seven microscopic thongs.

My three trips a week to Albertsons (now weirdly quiet with the shelves half empty—except for the beer and wine aisle) were racking up an impressive balance. The fridge was overflowing with eggs, bacon, Kirkland margaritas, DoorDash leftovers (you had better hide these if you didn't want them to disappear to the 2 a.m. eaters) and all our screw-top grape favorites.

Evenings were spent playing Dominoes and Quiplash (we found out later this game got a whole lot juicier after Tom and I went to bed), eating homemade popcorn loaded with parmesan, watching bad documentaries (even I got sucked into *Tiger King*), doing puzzles, baking cookies and—you name it—any activity that paired well with wine.

On warm days, we might start the festivities at noon, with an Aperol Spritz by the pool. Because, why not? Anything to drown out the unspoken fear of "We're all gonna die anyway!"

Actually, we did have a lot of fun with this in the beginning.

Our first annual StageCouch Music Festival, held in the backyard with eight rowdy attendees, was a rousing success. With custom signage stretched between two patio umbrellas, a fully stocked Beer Garden and VIP lounge with made-to-order cocktails, it was the perfect remedy for our terminal boredom.

But with a houseful of family to feed and water that had nowhere to go, it eventually felt like every day was a festival Saturday and *Did I just finish that whole bottle?* became my uneasy norm.

I was never falling-down drunk or anything. It wasn't like that. I didn't drive if I'd been drinking, so there were no DUIs or car accidents. I never drank in the morning. (Unless of course it was a weekend, holiday, my birthday, or *insert special event here.*)

There was just a slow IV of wine that usually started around five o'clock and continued until bedtime, when I poured myself to sleep.

On the outside, I moved through my usual routine. Running, working, cooking, entertaining, traveling when we could (*getting on an airplane requires no excuse for drinking!*), and caring for our home.

*Nothing better than a glass of wine to motivate me to get that pantry organized!*

Short-tempered and grumpy all the time, I wondered where my happy-go-lucky self had gone. Most mornings I woke up feeling disgusted with myself, but too embarrassed and ashamed to admit it.

When had cocktail hour changed from being fun to an exhausting chore? An obligation?

*Did I have a drinking problem? Nah.*

Instead, I became adept at adjusting my life to accommodate regular hangovers—never scheduling any appointments before eleven in the morning.

*I'm not a morning person.*

On many occasions, I attempted to moderate, promising myself I was only going to have one (or two) glasses of wine tonight. NO MORE.

*I want to feel good tomorrow.*

(And two glasses of wine is nothing. Practically like having water!)

Inevitably, after the first glass, my resolution went out the window.

*I'll skip wine tomorrow*, I decided as the pale-yellow gold filled my oh-so-pretty wineglass.

Attributing my bleary state of misery every day to getting older, I continued to gaslight myself. I knew if I admitted I was drinking too much, I'd have to give it up—and there was absolutely no way I was going to do that.

Not drinking was only for alcoholics, Mormons, and weirdos!

*Am I an alcoholic?*

Consulting Google for a diagnosis, I was surprised to discover that having more than one five-ounce drink seven days a week put me in "heavy drinker" status.

*What? This is surely fiction.*

First of all, I didn't know anyone who poured a five-ounce glass of pinot grigio. I didn't know anyone who poured a five-ounce glass of anything.

 Certainly not my bartender.

And drinking more than one teeny, tiny glass a day made me a LUSH? That's ridiculous! Everyone I know drinks more than this.

And truthfully, one glass of wine has never been enough for me.

As spring approached, rules banning large gatherings in California were being eased, so Tom and I decided to try and squeeze in a small backyard wedding.

The thought that I probably needed to take a break from alcohol still hovered in the back of my mind, but I knew for a fact that I would not be skipping prosecco at my own nuptials!

In fact, we came up with our own signature cocktail—The TNT— a spicy Paloma with tequila, red grapefruit juice, soda, blue agave nectar, and a tahini rim. I heard it was a hit with our guests, but I stuck with champagne just to be safe.

I wanted to remember our special day.

We didn't offer anything special for our non-drinking guests beyond water, soda, and sparkling juice. It never once occurred to me to do a festive drink for our guests who didn't imbibe. (Drinkers have a one-track mind.)

My heart overflowed as I walked between my parents down our makeshift aisle toward Tom, who beamed at me from under the flower-covered arch. Our six children stood and turned to watch us approach, their expressions a mixture of tender smiles and silent tears as they watched their parents prepare to marry new life partners.

Traveling after our wedding was still difficult, but we took a trip to Maui anyway, as our "unofficial honeymoon." Rental cars were scarce and dinner reservations in Lahaina were impossible. Instead, we strolled from our beachfront condo to pick up wine at a nearby market and dinners from food trucks. Dining from recyclable cartons on our balcony, we relished the warm evenings and the sounds of waves crashing on the shore below.

Each of my morning hangovers was gently soothed by a piña colada, mai tai, or glass of wine by lunchtime, so all was—a little shaky—but well.

The notion that I needed to take a break from alcohol had not gone away. But I just couldn't get myself TO DO anything about it.

There always seemed to be another exciting event coming up so I kept holding out—hoping, praying, wishing (and pretending) that maybe I was wrong. Because, well, I REALLY liked wine.

The highlight of summer was a weeklong Florida vacation with all the kids, endless White Claws, and the rest of the United States population. It seemed the whole world was pining for a tropical getaway after being stuck at home for so long.

We packed in a boatload of good times in the adorable gulf coast town of Destin, barely making it out of there as Tropical Storm Fred barreled toward us.

After changing airports to better our odds for departure, we ended up stuck for eight hours in Panama City Beach—the tiny airport running on backup generators—the lights in the terminal wavering on and off, freaking out many in our travel party. (Okay, mainly me.)

My biggest prayer—a close second to flying home safely—was that they didn't run out of those little bottles of cheap white wine I was chugging in the one and only bar. I talked the bartender into stashing a couple of them away for me, just in case.

After we got home, I felt that exhausted and terrible "I need a vacation from my vacation" feeling.

Unpacking my bags, I was shocked to find a receipt from the airport bar shoved to the bottom of my carry on, totaling over $900. Most of the tab was for Barefoot Pinot Grigio.

The signature scrawled at the bottom was impossible to read but I knew it was mine.

# There's No Right Way

## Saadia Ali Esmail

"Dads love like no other." The simple rectangular frame, the words inscribed in a whimsical font with gold lettering, next to a printed picture of a smiling father. His side pose reveals the defined features of his crinkled eyes, his straight nose, his jawline hidden behind his stark white beard, his silky salt-and-pepper hair neatly combed save for a few strands gathered around the top of his ear. A grandfather caught in the middle of a laugh; his lips parted just enough to let out the sound of his usual chuckle. Except it is now a sound of silence, the echoes reverberating within the limits of my memory, fading into a hushed void.

My neighbors across the street presented me with this frame on the one-year anniversary of my father's death this past Halloween. A "reverse" trick-or-treat, they called it, in which they rang the doorbell and gave me this treasure, receiving nothing in return save for a heartfelt embrace, a tearful appreciation. I wonder if there is a similar frame to this, one in which the inscription reads, "Daughters love like no other." I'll remember to look for one and set it by his grave next time I visit him.

I sat down on my sofa last night, legs outstretched and covered with a plush Costco throw, intending to revise a chapter from my book draft in time for my R&C class the following afternoon. My eyes glanced around the room and settled on this frame instead. And my fingers froze for a few minutes as I took in the picture of my father, probably one of his last happy moments captured through the lenses.

It's been almost seventeen months since he passed away. The "time will heal" advice that I received so often last year has become less frequent now, replaced with "You will smile at his memory soon." Both are still lies. I have not "healed" in any capacity; I have just learned to live with a hollowness that has shaped itself into an invisible scar. And my pretend smile gets pasted for the world to see whenever his name comes up as I busy myself with some mundane task to avoid the sudden burn that stings, its embers engulfed in the salt of my unshed tears.

I know I'm not alone, not in the world, for everyone has experienced grief in some form, nor at home. My three kids, each in their own respective ways, bring him up wistfully, in memories, in wishes, in "if onlys." And only now do I understand their method of grief, whereas before, I had not fathomed that they had harbored so much.

This evening is my son's Misaq, a coming-of-age event in our sect of Islam, not dissimilar to the Jewish Bar Mitzvah or the Catholic Confirmation, in which he will promise to uphold the tenets of our faith. No small milestone. I know my father is looking down, blessing him, celebrating with us—as my son is his only grandson in the midst of four granddaughters. When he was a young child, Humza had insisted on finding and gifting his Nana with a mug that said, "World's Best Grandpa," a vessel my dad used daily for his afternoon tea. For weeks, when Amazon was not something he was comfortable ordering from, my father drove to endless Hallmark stores in search of a "Best Grandson" mug to return his heartfelt sentiments. Even today, my son will not voice his sadness at losing his grandfather, keeping his feelings to himself as many a typical teenage boy does.

My oldest daughter turns eighteen in May. For her birthday, she asked if she could get a tattoo. "I could get one with Nana's name or his signature, a small one so he is always with me," she says with a sigh.

As her graduation draws nearer, she lists all the things she wants to do, never missing a chance to say, "If only Nana was here. I had all these plans with him after graduation." We'll keep an empty seat next to us on the bleachers with his picture, enlarged, smiling at Zahabiya as she walks to get her diploma.

And my youngest daughter loves to flip through the Memory book on my nightstand, or to finger his photo on that frame that sits on display in our living room. A few days ago, she came up to me while

I was cooking dinner in the kitchen, and took my hand to stop me for a few seconds.

"You know that day when I was on the horse, and Ms. Kristie told me to balance, holding my arms out wide? I was so scared that I would fall off, but you know what? Then I imagined Nana's hands holding my back, and I did it perfectly!"

And then she enveloped me in a bear hug. She has no doubt that her dear grandfather will always hold her; she was his favorite hugging grandkid.

It's a rainy day today in otherwise sunny San Diego. The last few weeks, whenever it has rained, I have felt dismal, missing my father even more, my tears mixing with the raindrops, some as mist, others as big droplets. There is such a thing as complicated grief—as if grief could ever be simple. But there are levels of it, and I'm thankful that I'm not in the "complicated" category where I could easily have gone down the abyss of depression at the loss of my father. Especially with my past episodes of depression, feelings of hopelessness triggered by hormones, or things I can still not identify.

Rather than saying, "I'm sorry for your loss," or "Time will heal," or the many other clichéd phrases most people have said in these last several months, helpful or otherwise, I wish they had instead remained silent. Or told me to have patience with myself. As my husband told me this morning, when I cried, I couldn't do anything except think of my father.

"Forget about this work and that work and the list of things you need and want to do. Take this day, use it for writing or missing your father or just sitting." In other words, deal with it as only I can. With patience for myself and my feelings. I cannot fight them, I can just accept them without a timeline or a schedule or any advanced warning. Let them in, let them hover around, let them leave. And the cycle will repeat because grief is anything but linear.

# If You Just Do This or You Just Do That, Everything Will Be Fine

## Amy Strommer

Once upon a time, a girl with flaxen hair and steely blue eyes entered this world to parents who loved her more with every breath she took. They caressed her toes and tickled her chin. The baby looked at the world that welcomed her with an intensity and awareness beyond her age.

And people said: "Oh, what a cute baby! She is so alert and observant. You are so fortunate."

And they were right.

And they were wrong.

The baby grew into a little girl. She looked at the world around her with interest and doubt. She heard the wind gathering in the distance and saw shadows in the corners. And the girl whimpered.

And people said: "If you just do this and if you just do that, then everything will be fine."

But it wasn't.

As the girl grew, she watched the white doves land in the trees and heard their gentle coos. But as the girl took an innocent breath, a blackness filled the sky, and the white doves disappeared. The girl cried and looked at the world with fear.

And people said: "If you just do this and if you just do that, everything will be fine."

But it wasn't.

The girl grew taller and ventured into her child world, finding others who looked like her. She heard their laughter and watched their easy play. She looked at her world with questions and apprehension. She did not laugh, and she did not play.

And people said: "If you just tell her this and if you just tell her that, everything will be fine."

But it wasn't.

The girl became a young lady and learned a wealth of knowledge without trying. She drew and painted like the ancient masters. She created beauty alone in her world.

The young lady heard the wind gaining strength and saw the shadows moving closer, but no words of worry or questions arose from her mouth. She kept her insides sealed.

And the people said: "If you just do this and you just do that, everything will be fine."

But it wasn't.

And as she grew, she became like a volcano—fiery, angry, and dangerous—but no words of connection or requests for help left her mouth. She kept her storm to herself.

But her parents saw the volcano simmering. They heard the rumbles. They felt the fire under the surface.

And the parents said: "If we just do this and we just do that, everything will be fine."

But it wasn't.

The years walked along, and the young lady became a woman. She suffered the inhumane heat inside her volcano and glared at the threatening shadows. She felt great fear in her volcano world. And the volcano became more than she could bare. She needed release.

And the people said: "If you take this and you take that, you can make the storm go away."

And she did what they said.

And she took it.

For just a moment, there was nothing.

And that felt good.

The woman tried to hide in her volcano from the gale-force winds and the darkness greater than herself. But sometimes, in the quiet of the night, she wished and hoped to find her way out of the storm. But the path forward held rose bushes with gigantic thorns waiting to hurt her every move. The path backward contained shadows, darkness, and pain. She remained inside.

And the people said: "Take this and take more of that and drink this and drink more of that, and everything will be fine."

And it wasn't fine.

But she didn't hear the gale-force winds.

And she didn't see the black shadows beckoning her.

And her brain was quiet for a moment.

Until it wasn't.

The woman listened to all the people who did not know her or care for her or love her but who took away her pain with what felt like magic. But it wasn't magic. It was poison.

And she sat in her volcano.

The storm brewed above her. The heat from within scorched her.

And her parents said: "Please, oh please, just do this and don't do that, and everything will get better."

But the pain of the storm was too much.

And she hid inside with no way forward and no way back, only venturing out for more poison to numb her world.

Once upon a time, a baby girl was born to parents who loved her more with every breath they took. The baby became a woman in what seemed like overnight, and this woman looked at them with an intensity and awareness beyond her age.

And people said: "Oh, your daughter is brilliant and anxious and fearful and strong and dark and creative and stubborn and funny and hurt and suffering. But she is still here."

And they were right.

And they were wrong.

# Friending My Brother

## Michelle Goering

On the anniversary of my brother's death, Facebook suggested him as a friend. We never connected online; he was in a non-friend category in my mind, when I allowed him headspace at all.

It was hard to talk to Darin, and hard to see him. He was in Texas, dying over decades, of alcoholism. He drunk-called me to cry and laugh about his losses—his wife, his daughter who was done talking to him, his job, his health. I had little to offer; I was swimming hard in my own messy life, and letting him in hurt.

I'd pushed him away for years. But here was a trace of the time I'd missed.

I clicked on his account. Job Status: Self-Employed. I knew he'd been fired. Educational Institution: The School of Hard Knocks. I smiled. I didn't recognize any of his friends. He'd posted photos of his pit bull Rosie, plugs for his San Antonio Spurs, and short quips:

*I don't always listen to AC/DC, but when I do, so do the neighbors.*

*Every day that I live and get older, I hate summer just a little more.*

Rosie died before Darin. He shot her after her back was shattered by a car. He had no money for a vet and was too drunk to drive her to one. On the phone, he said, "It was the hardest thing I've ever done." He wanted to shoot himself then, too, but said: "I couldn't do that to Mom."

I stopped scrolling when I saw an old photo of Darin and his friend Jeff on a tricycle. Darin is driving. Jeff stands behind him on the rusty trike's platform, his hands on Darin's shoulders. The caption says, "Here's the true meaning of best friends for life. Jeff even trusted me when we were four."

I lean in. Darin stares back, his body coiled for takeoff. The photo is fuzzy, but I can fill the gaps. I know the blue of his eyes, his white-blond hair, the space between his teeth. I feel his hands in mine, his body vibrating with a wild energy. I rejoiced to have a brother when we adopted him, a playmate and cure for my loneliness. Looking back, I see signs that he would break all our hearts—that we'd be unable to love him enough.

My heart twists—not for his death, but for our distance. If I had a do-over, I'd friend him on Facebook. Not to say the unsaid, and not to try to lengthen his life by even one day.

I'd "like" his comments, and share posts about Stephen King and Lee Childs, about bacon-laden breakfasts, about our Mennonite hometown. We'd share Mom's decline, and sit with the truth of Dad's violence. I'd share photos of my twins, his nephews.

And I'd give Rosie a thumbs up, though I'm afraid of pit bulls. Four days before he died, Darin changed his profile picture to hers. She gazes at me, her blocky heart-shaped face turned up. *I'm a good dog*, she pleads. *I am. You would've loved me, if we had ever met.*

# The Conversation Notebook

## Janet Travers

The dreariness of the morning cast its spell on Theresa as she prepped for her biweekly phone call to her mother, Alice. Alzheimer's disease had been the tortoise in the race, but changed into the hare, quickly taking over full-time residence in her mother's brain two years ago. Theresa made coffee and then kicked some roundhouses to her son's punching bag. She had to call her mother at the nursing home before 11:00 am EST, after breakfast but before lunch when her mother was allegedly most lucid. If she didn't call at exactly the right time, their so-called conversations made even less sense.

Theresa traced the beginning of her mother's decline to ten years ago when she began making irrational statements and acting paranoid. The first incident she noticed was when Alice thought Theresa's then two-year-old son was trying to hurt the gardener's daughter, who was watching her father mow the lawn. Alice had screamed out the front window of her house at the boy to leave the girl alone. Theresa's son had been trying to play with the girl when he heard his grandmother yell at him, and he began to cry. Theresa consoled him, then sat with her mother, and told her she shouldn't have done that; the children were just playing. Her mother made a harumph sound and walked away.

During the same visit, Theresa was leaving for the grocery store when her mother got angry and stated she didn't appreciate deliberately being left behind. "Of course, I want to go into town," her mother said, "I'm not going to sit and rot around here all day. Where's my pocketbook?" Then the hunt for her pocketbook ensued. When they got to the store, Alice took items off shelves and said things like, "Well, would you look at that," or "I've never seen tuna in a can before in my life." Initially, this was entertaining. They shopped for about an hour, Theresa following her mother around returning every fascinating item to the shelf from which it came.

Theresa readied herself for these phone calls by placing what she called her "conversation notebook" and pen to her left and a coffee and cigarette to her right. She used to put makeup on during these conversations, but inevitably, she'd smear her eyeliner every time because she couldn't be witty and patient while trying to draw a line on her eyelid. Her crutch was the five drags of a cigarette she permitted herself to have. She hid a cigarette pack a while back for certain occasions. The staleness of the cigarettes discouraged her from becoming a full-time smoker again. Counting the drags, she wrapped up the conversation after five.

She went outside and sat at the patio table, zipped her jacket, propped her head on her fist, stared at the phone number on her cell phone, and called.

"Village Nursing Center, how can I help you?" the receptionist asked in a heavy New York accent. Whenever Theresa heard that accent it either comforted her because it sounded like home, or it reminded her that she moved away a very long time ago and didn't belong there anymore.

"Yes. Hello. This is Theresa Moynihan. May I please speak with Alice Moynihan in Unit C?"

"Hold please."

Unfortunately, the precursor to every conversation while on hold was recorded Muzak. Finally, a nurse answered the phone. Theresa lit the cigarette and took her first drag.

"This is Theresa Moynihan; may I please speak to Alice Moynihan? I'm her daughter."

"Sure, hang on." Theresa started doodling on a new page in the conversation notebook. After a few minutes, the nurse got back on the line, and said to Theresa's mother, "Here Alice, this is your daughter, Theresa."

"Here Alice. This is your daughter, Theresa," Alice repeated into the phone.

"Hi, Mom. I'm Theresa. I'm your daughter. How are you?" Her mother paused, and as was her way, started reading aloud anything she set her eyes on.

"This … is not … a junk drawer. This is not a junk … this is not a junk drawer."

"I know you're sitting at the nurses' station, right, Mom? Do they have that written on a drawer in front of you? We all have junk drawers. I like mine. It's like a treasure chest. You put stuff in it when you don't know where else to put it, then you open the drawer another day and find all sorts of surprises."

"Two through four," her mother continued. "Two through for-ty. Twenty-one to forty. Wait.…"

"I think those are the numbers on the wall to let you know where rooms are."

"Yes, twenty-one to forty. This is not … a junk drawer."

"How are you today, Mom? This is Theresa, your daughter. Did you have breakfast? Did it taste good?"

"Yes, the food is good. Can you hear that?" Theresa heard a loud beeping in the background. She knew it was the alarm set off when one of the inmates attempted to get out of their wheelchair.

"Yes, I can hear that, Mom. Keep the phone to your ear. Let's ignore the beeps while we talk for a few minutes. You said your breakfast tasted good?"

"Yes, good, the food is very good, this is not a junk drawer."

"So, it's nice here in California. That's where I live, for a long time. It's finally getting cool. What's the weather like there? Is it raining?"

"It's white. It's surrounding. It's quiet. What do you call it? It's … Happy Birthday!"

"Happy Birthday to you, too! Happy almost Christmas, Mom. It must be snowing outside. Snow is white. Merry Christmas."

"Yes. This … is not a drunk, this is not a junk drawer."

"What color are your shoes? Do you have shoes on?"

"Can you hear that?"

Alice had to take her phone calls at the nurses' station so they could keep an eye on her. In a way, it was the cool place to hang out, like teenagers meeting at a pizza joint, a lively buzzing area.

A woman started screaming in the background and Theresa could hear the attendants try to calm her. Theresa took her second hit off her cigarette. Her neck started to hurt so she rolled her head from left to right. When Theresa visited the nursing home after her mother was first admitted, she pushed Alice in her wheelchair to a window of the dismal, mauve-colored visiting room. Her mother's head was bent down to her chest, so Theresa massaged her shoulders. Alice seemed to enjoy it, but a part of her brain must have reminded her that she didn't like to be touched. Without moving, she said, "That's enough."

Going over family history was pointless. Talking about the weather was meaningless, current events a waste of time. When she spoke to her mother, she rolled the dice and crapped out.

"This is not a junk drawer."

"I know it's hard to talk with all that noise around you, Mom. This is Theresa, your vivacious, fabulous daughter, the one in California. Your favorite daughter, ha-ha. That was a joke. Keep the phone to your ear, Mom." Theresa couldn't hear her well, which usually meant she had dropped the phone into her lap.

"Mom. MOM. Pick up the phone and put it to your ear." Theresa took a third drag off the cigarette.

She heard a nurse's aide say to Alice, "No, don't try to get out of your chair. Here honey, put the phone to your ear. Your daughter wants to talk to you."

"Your daughter wants to talk to you," Alice said into the receiver.

"What color shoes do you have on?" Theresa asked again. She scored.

"One is white, one is red." Recently her mother had started kicking her shoes off and pulling her socks off with her toes.

"Mom, maybe you kicked off one of your shoes. Do you have one white sock on one foot and a red shoe on the other?" She cringed and cursed herself for asking too many questions at once.

"This is not a...."

Theresa finished her sentence for her, "... junk drawer." She took the fourth drag. "Okay, Mom. I love you."

"I love you too. Oh, I'm so glad to hear your voice," her mother said on the verge of tears.

"Mom, you know I'm Theresa, right?"

"This is not a...."

"I'll call again in a few days."

"This is not...."

"I love you, Mom."

"This...."

"Is there someone nearby who works there? Hand them the phone."

"Hey!" Theresa's mother yelled. "Stop all that nonsense. All this noise ... this is not a. ..."

"MOM, hand the phone to an aide." Theresa heard an attendant call to Alice.

"Hallelujah!" Alice exclaimed and threw the phone to the ground. Theresa heard it bounce a few times.

The attendant picked up the phone. "Alice," she said, "don't try to get up. Don't pull your socks off—it's cold now. That's a good girl." The attendant spoke into the phone. "You know she didn't mean anything when she threw the phone. Say goodbye to your daughter, Alice."

Theresa's mother yelled into the phone. "Say goodbye to your daughter, Alice."

"Goodbye, Mom." Theresa took the fifth drag of her cigarette but didn't end the call. Sometimes the people in the nursing home would forget to disconnect the phone and she'd listen to her mother talking to whomever would listen. Someone would scream or laugh in the background, wheelchairs beeped. What she was hoping for was one day she would hear her mother say to the attendant, "Just kidding! I pulled a fast one on my daughter. Do you think she fell for it?" Or, "That's enough of this nonsense. Get my clothes and have someone drive me home."

Theresa looked at the circles she had drawn in her notebook during the phone conversation. Meaningless orbs clustered at the bottom of the page floated up and disappeared.

# Rain in Guanajuato

## Maria Zaragoza

Santiago Ibanez had always been a man of few words. One might even accuse him of being detached and aloof. Even as a boy, there was a stoicism about him that was unusual in a child. But in reality, Santiago considered himself to be a coward. He was afraid of showing the emotions he carried inside of himself and kept them bound, wrapped tightly around his chest like a terrible wound he could never leave unprotected for fear of it bleeding out.

Contrary to what people might assume, the reality was that Santiago felt things deeply. Too deeply, in his own opinion. He often felt suffocated by his emotions. They scared him. Paralyzed him so he couldn't speak, and it forced him to appear rigid and cold.

Even as a boy, he was always careful not to show too much. Because he knew if he did, everything he felt would spill out of him, and he'd be powerless to contain it again. He didn't want anyone to know the petrifying emotions he lived with day after day. He was already afraid of his own intensity—he did not need anyone else to fear him, too.

Because they would be afraid. They would be afraid of the anger he had carried around with him since his boyhood. His anger was one of his earliest memories. He was just shy of being five years old, and a group of men had ridden out to the farm where he had been born in Durango where he once lived with his mother and father.

"Please," Santiago remembered his father's voice. "This is our farm."

"Not according to this," one of the men said pulling out a document. "This land is officially vacant."

"We've lived here for generations. This was my father's land, and his father's before him—how can it just be taken from us?"

"You have no land anymore," another of the men said, forcibly shoving the document into his father's hands. "Now, this is your last chance. You know what happens to those who refuse to leave."

Santiago's father glanced at the men, who were already prepared with guns and ropes should he refuse anymore, then down at Santiago who was peeping behind his father's leg, and eventually nodded. "How much time will you give us?"

"Until sunset," they replied. "We'll be back then."

*Sunset*, Santiago remembered thinking. *What are we to do then?*

When the men left on their horses, and they could barely be seen over the horizon, Santiago's father looked at the document in his hand and cursed, "Damn judges." He muttered under his breath, "Damn Diaz. How—how's a man supposed—supposed to take care of his family when..."

"Papa," Santiago called to him then, "Papa, what did they want? Why do they want our farm?"

Mateo looked down at his son. "It's not ours anymore." He attempted to smile at him sadly, saying, "Come, we must hurry."

"But where are we to go?"

"I don't ... know, son." He quickly brushed the tears falling from his eyes and walked inside the house.

Santiago had never seen his father cry before. Not even when his mother had passed just a few months before. He decided then that he had to grow up. He must not ask questions, must not fuss, no matter how trying the journey was ahead. He followed his father inside the house and quietly packed his belongings. When the men came back on their horses, smirking and watching his father intently, the anger inside Santiago was born. He hated these men. Hated that they were taking his home away from him, hated that they had made his father cry. But he did not show it. He would not cause trouble for his father. He must act as a man now.

The anger stayed with him all through the long, weary journey from Durango to Guanajuato, where his father had been lucky enough to know of work. When they arrived in Guanajuato, they were hungry and tired, and his father had to sell small items to get food and a barn to rest their feet. Mateo had spent the first day in town asking anyone he could about work, and a small home for him and his son. It was fortunate for them when a kind, older woman took pity on them and told Mateo to look for work in the mines. As for a place to live, she knew there was a small piece of land available right next to hers. Mateo thanked the woman profusely and went with her to ask about it. Santiago was left on the side of the road, ordered not to move, and to guard their belongings and the few chickens they were able to bring with them.

Santiago, although scared, did not object to his father. He sat down on the dirt, playing and petting the chickens, until his father returned some long hours later. Mateo lifted his son into the cart with the chickens and began leading the way. Santiago wanted to hate Guanajuato. There were large haciendas and factories but everyone he passed by looked as weary and troubled as his father. He wondered if there were other men like the ones who took their farm here, too. Santiago wanted to go back home. He wanted his quiet, simple life back but he dared not open his mouth. Instead, he watched the road with a stern expression, mimicking the men he hated so much.

The only time Santiago let go of that anger was when he was with his best friend, Camila Marquez, the little girl who lived next door—and the granddaughter of the kind woman who had told his father about the land in the first place. They became close friends when Camila came to their house that day while his father was putting things inside. She had wanted to play with the chickens, but Santiago refused to let her. He did not want to risk losing them; he had already lost enough. Still, Camila was not deterred, and she asked to play with him instead. It had begun to rain and thunder heavily, and in an act of bravery, Santiago raced her back to her home, where her father was already looking for her. From that first day on, Santiago forgot all about hating Guanajuato, and he and Camilia became practically inseparable.

That was until they turned eighteen, and his anger, which he still always carried around with him like a thorn poisoning his side, led him to join Emiliano Zapata's Liberation Army. He did not tell anyone until the day before he was set to leave for Morelos. It had been raining that day as well, which he had thought was a shame. Rain reminded him of the first day he met Camila, and it was very special weather for him. He always thought of Camila when it rained.

When Santiago told her, he saw the anger in her face. He could not help but feel jealous. He wished he had her talent for expressing herself. With Camila, one always knew what she was feeling. It was written on her face always. He looked at her, her dark eyes and dark brows furrowed in frustration, and he wished he could tell her everything. He wished he could talk of his anger, his pain, and how he was joining Zapata to fight for a more just country so that no one else had to feel what he felt. But he could not. Camila gave him a cold goodbye, which pained him, but he did not protest. He considered it his price to pay for protecting her from himself.

He would not see Camila again for a few years. During his time in the army, he had made some enemies, and found himself going into hiding. Due to some confusion, the army believed him to be dead, and so they sent a letter informing his father. He was not made aware of this until years later when he was smuggled out of Mexico into the United States. He made his way to New Orleans. It had been the only city he could think of to go, since it reminded him of Benito Juarez. Once in the city, he wrote his first letter in quite some time to his father, stating that he was safe and in good health. He had just put the letter in the post when it began to rain. Santiago smiled to himself and prayed. He prayed for Camila and how he desperately wanted to see her again. It was then that she appeared before him. At first, he was certain it was only his imagination willing her face onto another woman's body, but it was indeed her, running to a hotel to get out of the rain.

He pulled his jacket over her, just like the first day they had met as children. When she turned to look at him, she appeared shocked, then angry. He tried talking to her but she would not let him and refused to listen. A man appeared suddenly, putting his arm around her, and led her away.

It made Santiago feel foolish. He had thought that if he ever saw Camila again, it would be just like old times. He would smile at her just as he always did and they'd be together just as they always had been. But he should have known better than anyone the way anger can take hold of a person. And Camila was angry. Why wouldn't she be? He had left her.

The image of the man putting his arm around her played repeatedly in his mind. It should not have surprised him, either. In the deepest, most profound areas of his heart, he knew he had been in love with Camila since they were children. It seemed, though, she did not feel the same. He could not fault her for this. In all their years of friendship, he had never been able to confess his feelings for her. Why would she ever love a coward like him? But when he saw that man put his arm on her shoulder, he wished he had told her everything. He wished—and not for the first time—that he could be articulate. A man of valor. A man so different from himself.

# Spinning Myself Back In

## Victoria Derr Valencia

I haven't deep cleaned my home since my lover left two weeks ago.

The intention? Fifty percent a tiny revolution of coming home to myself after a deep dive in someone else. The other fifty percent is wanting to keep some essence of him here: his toothbrush, my scrunchie he placed on a selenite spiral. One day, I'll pull the CAUTION plastic from the screen of my new car, like he urged me, as a revolt against this sterile perfectionism I've been taught is the peak.

Yesterday, I mopped the floor and a grief brought me to my knees. Sobs ran through my body. I allowed them to spill. Held my messy life in my hands. Admitted that deep cleaning the kitchen wasn't going to bring me certainty, or safety, or bone-deep knowing.

Attaching to the world of form brings immense grief—a pothos plant dies, a miscarriage ensues, you change apartments and towns and lovers, and nothing looks the same as it did seven years ago. Your very cells have changed in the last seven years.

The world behind form, the undying essence of all things—that is who to trust. That is who to look for when you're sobbing on the kitchen floor, overcome by the weight of uncertainty.

The temper tantrum ran through me. I know better than to shut my inner toddler up. I let her cry, let her tears stain her cheeks, let her howl. That's how we self soothe—through the throat.

Holding myself through it. Breathing myself through it. Reassuring myself I'm safe within it until I soften around it. Until it softens around me. Until I'm no longer crying or sniffling. Until I'm exasperated, laughing. Until I'm standing up to say,

"Knowing things is FUCKING OVERRATED," and continue mopping the kitchen.

I don't mop the hallway. I know better than to do too much at once. I fix a cup of tea. I stay with my breath. I stay with myself.

The kitchen is clean, the front door is shut. There are turkey meatballs in the fridge, and a warm cup of tea in my hands. I've returned to myself. Despite it all, despite the door being flung open and the uncertainty of a wild life and the lover who has left and the sobbing in the kitchen… despite it all, the altar candle is lit. Prayers have been said. My body continues to breathe. I hold myself through it. I return to myself.

One day, I'll peel the CAUTION plastic from the screen of my new car and allow myself to fully settle into the spaces I inhabit. Call myself home—an unmade bed, lemon zest on the counter, dishes in the Clorox-smelling sink. Learn the luxury of being lived in. And love the feeling—by God, love that feeling more than anything—the feeling of returning home to myself.

# Thawing

## Jamey Annette Fitzpatrick

"Your shoulder is frozen," the doctor says. It's as if he's talking about broccoli, or the weather outside. He's distant, amused with himself. "Sometimes that just happens." Now he actually smiles, "…especially with women, and you are in the right age range … thirty-five to sixty!" As if I have won a prize, at forty something. I can't raise my arm above my head, drive, use my mouse, or type without pain. But I fit his box. "We don't know exactly why it freezes, but eventually it becomes unfrozen." I resist telling him the word is "thaws." He and his nicely ironed chinos, too white smile, and white coat leave the room.

So when you left us, we went to your house. We spent several days—grief pushing us hard—to sort through your life. You are so much more organized than I will ever be. Clear boxes for Q-tips. Tiny colored boxes to sort the screws and the nails in the garage into different lengths for specific needs. No extra anything. Two sets of sheets for each bed. Back-up batteries for your electronics, a case that fits each, exactly. No papers that weren't needed. We kept looking, hoping to find a note somewhere, a postcard, a birthday card—something we'd sent to you. Something that connected us across time and space—those dotted lines between San Diego and Las Vegas and L.A. and back again.

We stood in your backyard and caught the sunset through your pine trees. Resting on the rocks you had moved back there, huge boulders where you relaxed and smoked, watching the pinks and oranges mix with the dark purple of the mountains in the distance. Nirvana in a Marlboro. The breeze blew softly, and I could almost smell the smoke on your black leather jacket, make out your phone's outline in your pocket. We stood where you stood, and there was some peace in that.

I was never sure when it was a good time to call. Sometimes I laughed so hard with you that my mouth hurt. When you were just happy or when you'd been smoking weed. Sometimes I just got off the phone with you and cried. Sorry for what I couldn't fix. You swinging between pain and euphoria and anger and calm, like the pendulum of an internal clock. We never knew quite what time it was, inside you.

You had a big, beautiful brain, slightly bruised here and there, like an apple under the trees of our childhood. It was always a toss-up who would answer the phone. A good day was wonderful. The bad days made me ache with a pain that can never heal. In any of us.

Today, I started off fine. Coffee, toast, and now my blue tennis shoes laced up. Out the door, the invisible force field broken through, cobwebs falling as I slip down the porch steps. Fifteen years ago I could have run six miles and never even thought about it. Now, I walk the blocks around our house within this pandemic border. What's safe anymore? Who are we if we can't stop and talk with the neighbor so worried she can't sleep? She drops off avocados later, and thanks us for the conversation. "I live alone," she says. "Sometimes it helps to get outside your own head."

You liked living alone, I think. I hope you heard the phone ringing that last day. That you knew how hard Mom was trying to reach you … the phone just kept ringing … thirteen different times. I emailed you, trying not to wake you. Neither of us dreamed how bad it was this time. The severe and sudden back pain was just one piece of the complex puzzle of your life.

I'm out looking for our lost cat and thinking of you. I'm shaking the treats with my bad arm, the frozen shoulder. It's been almost a month, but it feels like yesterday we lost him. Fourth of July. Idiots shooting off fireworks. Hundreds of cats and dogs ran away that weekend. I see flyer after flyer at the animal shelter and online. Little kids in the poster playing with their golden retriever now lost. Indoor cats that somehow got out. This stream of cats of every color running in my mind and on the streets—running in sheer terror—orange, tiger, black-and-white tuxedo, white, gray. Like you running from your past.

Ours was a little tiger cat with a big personality. He adopted us before the pandemic, and now is gone in the flash of a night.

If I could rewind time. Standing there, scratching his chin in the coming darkness, the faraway flash of fireworks began. He scoots away. Instead, in my dreams, I pick him up and take him inside. He'd be here on my lap now. Instead, I'm crawling under other people's houses peering into the darkness with a flashlight. Every bush is a possibility. Each car and tree a place to hide underneath or within. He was the kindest, gentlest little spirit. A reason to get up in the morning, even in the midst of these fearful, frantic times. He was hope with whiskers and a huge purr and he would run to us whenever he saw us coming. Lost in the aftermath of fire and flames in the sky and what must have felt like cannons blasting on the next street.

I am calling his name again and again as I walk, trying to hold back tears, hold onto the feeling of him in my arms. I hardly notice the figure walking next to me. In the stillness of the morning, I call. I undo my mask, so the sound will go further, into the backyards, through the gates, bringing him back through time and space. My mask dangles from one ear....

"Skittles ... Skittles!!! Here kitty, kitty.... Come here...."

"Listen to yourself ... you gotta sound like you can still find him ... not like he's gone forever." Taller than me, your voice is low and gravelly, like it always was, after your morning cigarette.

I stop. Swallow back the tears. The smoke hits me, but there's no one in the streets. I realize I do sound like I'll never find him again. I cry a little while walking next to you. It's good to stand near you. To know you are still here. Soon I hear my own voice, only stronger, solid, "Skittles!!! Here buddy.... Here kitty, kitty.... Skittles!!!

I see this lady peeking out her window as I walk by. I try to look less weird, feel less wild inside. Feel less like I've lost one of my best friends—again. Try to pretend I'm just taking a pretty walk in the quiet of morning. She looks out the window and has no idea who I am or what I am going through. Just tangled red hair, a sweaty freckled forehead, and a mask.

I am walking, tears slipping easily down my cheeks. I turn down our street, to the warm house waiting for me. There is another cat inside waiting for his belly to be rubbed. There is a beautiful woman who loves me and understands my sadness. And there is a life I have made.

Still some days, I am under that avalanche of snow. Frozen. February was so long that it felt like two months in Michigan. There are parts of me that will never thaw. My frozen shoulder is just the only piece the doctors can see. Something they can name, enter in my record, and walk away again.

One grief unleashes the fear and cold of other avalanches of past grief. Like a domino, they run into each other and knock more snow on top of you. I don't know what the worst part of grief is—who you've lost and knowing they will never come back, or all the broken pieces you have left in a pile—dreams, conversations, moments that fall before you like tiny stones in the snow. You scramble to pick them up and each one you touch is like ice, the sharp cold hurting the warmth of your hands, leaving tiny burns on your soft skin.

The last Christmas we had, that last hug you gave me before my partner and I got into the car to drive to L.A. You held me close, a really solid hug, and then when you started to pull away, I said, "Can I have another one? I never know when I'll see you again." You smiled a little, just the corners of your lips quivering, your black leather jacket crinkling as you held me again. Our last hug. We called you again when we got home to thank you for the amazing chocolate chip cookies you made us. It was the best Christmas in years, everybody able to hold it together. Enjoy time. Breathe. Laugh.

I remember telling you once the quote I'd heard that "the well-lived life was the best revenge." I hope that's where you are now. A place where it's always warm, and nothing ever freezes. No regrets, no pain, no loss. No need to drink. A body that's healed. And this lush island, with sandy shores filled with the sailboats you love. Enough quiet to think in. Floating there, bluegills beneath your boat, soft periwinkle sky stretching above. Whole again. Happy.

The mid-afternoon sun is melting through the snow now, and I finally see up. The blue of sky, a canvas above where I am laying, too. Pieces of you are still here, all around me. A seagull swooping in the wind. The stirring of the pine branches above. My eyelids keeping out the brightness of the sun. Still, I need its warmth. My red eyelashes, like yours, are staring up into the same blue. The sky, like me, is full, even if others can't see everything that is there. Everything that is thawing inside. I feel you beside me, smell your Marlboro, its traces like a mist rising toward the mountains.

# Aaron from OC

## Barbara Bowley

After a long first day in my new apartment, I sunk into my comfiest chair, propped my feet up on a moving box, and opened up my new dating app, a reward for all my labor.

A bright, hopeful couple smiled back at me as the app promised me "my last first date."

*Oh sure. Hinge—what kind of a name is that for a dating app? Sounds like something cooked up by a Silicon Valley incel. Okay, focus, focus. New apartment, new neighborhood. And hopefully—my new guy.*

I was presented with my first potential match, and my index finger hovered briefly before consigning him to his fate in my little online queendom. After a hundred or so matches, I started getting bored. *Keep looking, the needle in the haystack is out there.*

And then a photo caught my attention. It stood out from the long parade of hopefuls, partly because it was a crisp black and white, but more so because the subject couldn't have been more than thirty years old.

He had sent me a comment: "No way you're sixty-two. Gotta be a typo."

I swiped right so I could respond. "Not a typo. Thanks for the compliment! Best of luck."

I hit send, and immediately saw he was writing a reply. *Oh, jeez, he's online right now. Oops.*

"How do I get a date with someone as beautiful, experienced, and brainy as you?"

I felt a jolt, thinking it was time to jump off the site. But I steadied myself and typed, "That's sweet, but I'm looking for someone way closer to my age."

"Aw, I'm a lot of fun. Plus, I have young dad energy."

A photo began to materialize in the chat box. *Oh my God, please don't let this be a dick pic.*

It wasn't. He was bent over the engine of a bright red Mustang, looking up and showing off grimy hands and what seemed to be a carefully staged smudge on his right cheek. And that same carefree smile.

"Do you like a guy who's not afraid to get his hands dirty?" I smiled as he continued to type. "I'm a lot of fun. I'm different. No expectations, just some good conversation and vibes."

He sent his number. The Orange County area code meant he was over an hour away. *Nah.*

"Just a light chat," he persisted.

*Oh my god, what am I getting myself into? Maybe he'll get bored waiting for my answer, and hop off.* I imagined trying to explain this to my therapist … unsuccessfully.

"How's a chat now on Whatsapp?" he typed.

I took a deep breath. *Calm down, girl, it's just a video call.*

"Okay, Bryan, but I'm only free for about twenty minutes." My index finger felt like it belonged to someone else as I typed in my number.

"Hey, it's Aaron. Get it right!"

"Oh, I'm so sorry," I said. "I see it: 'Aaron from OC' is your profile name. How old are you again?"

"It's right there in my bio. I'm twenty-six. Are you checking out somebody else?"

*Twenty-six. Ten years younger than my stepson. Is he being creepy?*

"Okay, give me five," I said. I quickly looked at my image on the phone's camera, smoothed my hair, and grabbed a bit of tinted lip gloss. *God, I'm getting ready to look good for a twenty-six-year-old.* I almost hit the red hang-up button. Almost.

"Wow," he said with a genuine grin as we popped into each other's view. "You definitely look like your profile shots."

"I am very real and really sixty-two."

He talked about how he liked older women. Low drama and lots of confidence.

"I went out with a forty-year-old last month," he said.

It felt like I'd been hit with cold water. A forty-year-old woman would be old enough to be my daughter. "You don't look like sixty-two at all," he said. "You gotta tell me about your wellness routine."

Pretty soon I was hooked. Time flew as we compared notes on food and exercise, our pets, and our families. It had been fun and different, and as I tried to end the chat, he surprised me.

"Hey, I'd love to meet you. Are you free tomorrow?"

"Tomorrow?" I tried not to sputter. "No, I have stuff to unpack and boxes to move."

"Perfect. I'll help you move the boxes. I've got a strong back. And strong arms." He leaned back slightly in his chair, locking his hands behind his head, just shy of flexing.

"I need to know a lot more about you. Text me your last name, your LinkedIn profile ... and any watch lists you're on," I joked.

"You got it."

Aaron arrived at my apartment late the next afternoon, wearing a black T-shirt and jeans. He smiled as I let him in, and I noticed that he was a bit nervous. "Wow, nice place," he said. I put on some music and we got to work.

An hour later we were on the sofa, relaxing with a drink. "Thanks so much for your help," I said, genuinely grateful. "Hey, let's get some tacos in La Jolla while you tell me about life in the OC, young Aaron."

He looked pleased with himself, and at ease. "Awesome!"

When we got to my car, he flashed a grin. "Ooo-ee, this is a nice ride."

"Six-cylinder turbo," I said proudly. "You think you can handle it?"

He tossed me a look of mild disdain. "I'm a car guy!"

As I threw him the keys, the voice in my head said, "Complete stranger!" The damn killjoy sounded like my mom. I ignored her.

With the moonroof open and '90s hits belting out, he navigated us down the curves of Torrey Pines Road expertly, and just slightly too fast. As I glanced over at him, I suddenly realized that I was having long-forgotten feelings: young and on a date, with the world going by just a little too quickly, but everything being okay. *I'm sixty-two, and I can still feel this way. Wow.*

I took Aaron's arm as we arrived at the upscale restaurant. But when I glanced at all the young couples around us and realized how different we looked, my giddiness crashed. I dropped his arm, feeling as though it all might have been a mistake. *What if someone I know sees me with a guy this young?*

We sat at the bar and ordered. I vowed to lighten my mood. I turned to him and we smiled and clinked our margarita glasses together. In that moment, I realized simply that he was happy to be with me, and I was happy to be with him. I turned on the bar stool and our knees touched.

I tilted my head. "You know what this looks like? Like I'm paying you to be with me."

He smiled and winked. "Who gives a fuck?"

Laughing, I realized that young Aaron was right. Our two opinions were the only ones that mattered. *To anyone else who might care: You don't get to tell me how I should feel.*

I raised my glass in an appreciative toast and we chatted about online dating, about SoCal beaches, and whether San Diego or Orange County had better Mexican restaurants.

Later, when Aaron opened my car door for me outside the restaurant, I saw an incredible sight in the sky over his shoulder. Arching across the night sky was what looked like a trail of golden, glittering dust. I pointed and said, "It's a shooting star! We have to make a wish!"

He slipped an arm around my waist and pulled me to his side. Full of wonder, I felt like a teenager for the second time that night.

Back at my place he gave me the lightest of kisses and I wished him goodnight. The next morning, he texted me that he'd had a great time, and sent a local news link about what we'd seen. It turned out that our late-night shooting star was actually the launch of a SpaceX satellite. I had to laugh.

I texted him, "It sure seemed real at the time! I made a wish anyway."

He replied, "So did I," with a heart emoji.

We texted on and off for the next couple of weeks until life took us elsewhere.

I never got to say thank you, so I'm doing it now. Aaron, thank you for making me feel seventeen again. For showing me that some things between men and women are timeless.

These days I'm looking for a man my age who can make me feel the way Aaron did. Because I know that feeling is still in me, and I know there's a guy out there who wants to feel that way too. *Thank you, Aaron from OC, all of twenty-six. You're gonna make a great young dad someday. How do I know? Because I'm a woman of experience. And because that's what I wished for you.*

# A Place Called Home

## Cherie Kephart

This isn't my story. I found it by accident. Or serendipity. You can decide.

It came to me in January. Sitting in my living room, I could see discarded Christmas trees on the street below. Once they stood tall, verdant, and were cherished centerpieces of homes. Now, they slumped, lifeless against the pavement, dried and unloved.

The haunting stillness and silence of the castoff trees sent a shudder through me. In the browned needles I saw the reflection of where I believed my life was now. Used. I wondered what was next for me. Had anything I had done mattered? I crafted words into pages, some read, appreciated even, and some left in drawers and deep in computer files that no eyes other than mine would ever see.

I shook my head like I was trying to dislodge the melancholy thoughts out through my ears. Turning my attention back inside my living space, I grabbed my cell phone and called the new water-delivery service I was signing up for. I heard two rings, then a cheery male voice said, "Hello! How can I help you today?"

A wave of delight surged inside me. This guy sounded so joyful. "Hi," I said. "You always answer the phone this upbeat?"

"Yes. Of course. I'm a happy guy."

"Oh yeah?" I smiled, feeling uplifted by his enthusiasm. "What makes you so happy?"

He chuckled. "It's because I know my life purpose."

I didn't know what to expect, but I was curious. I inserted my earbuds, preparing to hear better whatever was coming next. "So, you going to tell me?"

His mirthful tone grew, and he spoke as if he recited a scientifically verified truth. "My life purpose is to hold on to different things until someone who needs them comes along."

"Huh?" Not the answer I was expecting.

His cadence quickened. "I'm a fixed point in reality, a placeholder. It may be a monetary thing; it may be a piece of information. It could be anything, but everything I have in my life, I'm a placeholder for."

I listened while pacing down the hallway, my bare feet nestling in the rough carpet. My cat Jade glared at me like I was expending precious energy and should consider taking a nap.

The man continued. "It's like a perpetual Pay It Forward kind of thing. Skills, knowledge, friendship. I've got it to give. I have side quests too, but this is the main one. 'Here's a car, I don't need it because I have two. You need it so you can get to your job, so take it.'"

"Fascinating." I imagined this unseen man: dark hair, big brown eyes, and an aura of affable bravado lingering around him.

"It's normal to me." He cleared his throat, then described how it played out in his everyday world, being gifted and finding things only to give them away—helping people find jobs, giving people rides, leaving money on the street so someone could find it. After ten minutes he stopped talking, like an alarm sounded and our time was up. I heard his hearty laugh. "Guess we should get you some water."

Shaken out of the world he'd brought me into, I'd forgotten where and why I was even calling. "Ah, sure."

"How about we start with your name?"

"I'm _____."

"Hi _____, I'm Manuel."

I wanted to know more. Why he felt so certain and strong about his purpose and where it came from. I wondered if I'd ever been that certain about anything in my life.

After I ordered my water service, we exchanged numbers and agreed to continue our conversation on Sunday. For the next three days, one question plagued me: What was my purpose? I had always pondered it and yet never quite reached a quenching answer.

Sunday afternoon arrived and Manuel called me on cue. His voice came wild and loud. "Hey. You ready?"

I didn't waste a moment. "Absolutely."

I walked over to Jade on her kitty perch and stroked her tortoise-shell colored fur. Her motor roared and Manuel's voice barreled at me with gusto. "When life happens, and someone needs something, I give it to them. I used to get frustrated that I would lose things that came to me, but then. . . ." I heard him take a breath. "It's easy for me to give now and give things up because I know what it means to not have. And to need."

"What happened?"

Then it came out, bursting from the phone.

"I was on the streets. Homeless. With my mom. We had nothin'."

I slid down onto the floor, my body a lump against the couch cushion.

"When I was sixteen, my ma got sick from asbestos. She barely survived. I worked at fast-food restaurants to support us, but it wasn't enough. I became a facilitator for getting weed to friends, via the drive thru. But it got out of hand real quick. I couldn't care for my ma if I was in jail. So, I stopped dealing, but I could no longer pay our rent."

I closed my eyes and heard his voice sink deep into my being.

"We didn't have anywhere to go. Our family wouldn't even take us in. My grandma gave me a blanket and fifty bucks. My aunt gave us two nights in a motel. I was too embarrassed to ask for help from my friends.

"One day my ma and I were wandering around the beach, trying to find a place to sleep. I saw a dolphin in the water and thought, *If we're goin' to be homeless, why not at the beach?* Homeless in Oceanside."

I didn't have any words to match his. It didn't matter because Manuel kept delving further into the cavern of his past.

"We learned quick how to survive. It's a few degrees warmer at the end of the pier when it gets cold. And we found out a lot about laws. Best thing I learned is that the cops can't arrest you if you have a fishing pole in your hand. Get a fishing pole on the pier, they can't do anything to you. I didn't like fish, but I ate it. I was hungry."

I glanced at my kitchen. Nothing lavish since I was sort of a minimalist. But I had much more than one person needed. A pang of guilt coursed up my body.

"Being homeless became easy after a while," he continued. "Cold food. Cold body. Time's irrelevant. All you're doing is livin'. And you're out of the cage. Trapped in freedom. But there's a price you pay for that kind of freedom, the type that is thrust upon you. Society rushing on while you exist on the sidelines.

"My ma and I were close before this, but we became best friends. I tried to get a job, yet when I was gone, she got jumped. Teenagers busted her lip, broke a tooth, and took her blanket. Two times on the street she almost died. I had to protect her, so I couldn't leave her anymore. We'd just have to stay homeless.

"And we never once asked people for change. We didn't ask anybody for anything. But that water, that kept us alive."

Hearing his words, I was transported to the ocean tide. The impermanence and grandeur of it all. How small I feel next to it. How it always feels like I could be swallowed up and never seen again in the time of a wave.

His voice roared, knocking me out of my reverie. "But the answer to life is not at the water," he said. "Or in the cage. A situation is just that. A situation. Nothing more. It's about being like water. Fluid. Buoyant. Rollin' with whatever comes your way." He paused. "Even though I lived this, I often need the reminder."

Tears filled my eyes. "Don't we all."

He paused once again, then spoke. "After eighteen months, my ma and I climbed our way back into four walls 'cause of the generosity of a girl I met at the library. Her family had an apartment complex and they took us in. Soon, the tick-tock of structure began again. But on our terms. We knew who we were and where we'd been."

The beauty of his words ignited tremors of hope. I leaned my head back, closed my eyes, and let his voice continue to guide me.

"It's fifteen years later and I have an apartment, a job, a wife, my mom is in better health, and I have my friends, and that's where I hold value. I don't value things. They're great to have. And great to give to people in need. There's a difference between someone needing something and wanting something.

"People get caught up. . . . The world has been conditioning us that we're victims, but we're not. Ultimately, we're powerful beings. How we handle a situation and what we do is what matters."

His voice sounded overused. Parched.

A sense of optimism replaced the hollowness I had previously suffered. "Manuel, your life is beautiful. Where you've been and who you are."

"Thanks. But it's just me. I'm not afraid of being homeless now—I'm not afraid of losing stuff. I know what I'd do. I feel fortunate. It was one of the most important times of my life."

After three hours, I thanked him for letting me into his world, for exposing the rawest parts of who he is. He simply said, "No problem. I've got it to give."

I hung up the phone. My ears were hot from the earbuds. My brain blurred from all the details he shared. I rose from my position sprawled on the carpet, wiped my tears with my sleeve, and walked out onto my balcony, breathing in the fresh midday air. I looked onto the hill adjacent to the lake and a lanky blue heron took flight. His expansive wings moved in surges of purity and grace, his long body reflected in the whispering navy water beneath the sunlight. I wondered what I had to give.

In a flash, I felt it. What had just transpired. Manuel was right. His life purpose was to be a placeholder. He held on to his story until the right person came along. For I collect stories.

As I said, this isn't my story. But now, just like Manuel, it has a home.

# Poetry

*The oppressed must see examples of vulnerability of the oppressor so that a contrary conviction can begin to grow within them.*

—Paulo Freire

At a time when white supremacy is visible and accepted, artists must remind themselves of not only the power of their art, but also the responsibility that comes with owning their craft.

The artists you are about to read hold their truths in an infrastructure that does not promote art as resilience. Resistance cannot exist without oppression. A revolution cannot exist without resistance from its artists.

When civilians are in a state of fear, we turn to artists. For this pernicious country does not hold truth to its liberations and freedom for all. In reality, it's a prejudicial structure where white supremacy thrives and continues to insert itself in a racial hierarchy. That is, until art takes over.

Art is specific. Art is complex. Art will dismantle the ideology of superiority as we are reminded that our inner artists are always the solution, that we ourselves are not part of the social justice movement but we ARE the social justice movement.

Art rejects white supremacy.

Art rejects oppression.

Art rejects patriarchy.

Art rejects homophobia.

Art rejects sexism.

Art rejects fascism.

Art rejects our children in cages.

Art rejects the incarceration of men and women of color.

Art rejects the genocide of poor people.

When artists disrupt forms of oppression from the courtroom to the classroom, we begin the process of liberation for all. A critical reflection of self is required so we understand each other because nobody is truly liberated by themselves. And such liberation requires an artist to be responsible because it is art that transforms us back to being human.

—Vera Sanchez, M.Ed
Poetry Editor, *A Year In Ink, Volume 18*

# Epilogue for a Poem

## Lucy Lehman

It began with
    a stray thought
an inspiration conceived,
    a theme hatched
like a snail in a shell
    snug in its whorls
a poem germinating until ready
    to emerge in stanzas
of transcendent verse.

I begin to write,
    at first inspired,
but then aware
    that I'm far from
the first poet facing the challenge
    of translating
the ephemeral
    into words.

Like an old magician
    who dares perform
a hackneyed magic trick,

I fear my poems
will be compared
   to the old masters',
whose works are revered.


Aware then that my hatchling
   might not survive
the scrutiny of critical eyes,
   my inspiration falters.
I put down my pen
   and wonder:
*what if I fail to find the right words?*
   *Should I even try?*

Afraid my hatchling poem
   might not survive
the scrutiny of critical eyes,
   my inspiration falters.
I put down my pen, sigh,
   and ask myself
dare I try?

# Culture Shock

### Claire Hsu Accomando

I tell my mother I want a purple dress.
*Purple is cheap*, she says.

*It's a color that screams*
*look at me, look at me.*

But purple is pretty.
*You look better in blue.*

*It's not show-offy.*
*You want to look elegant.*

*You want to be noticed for what*
*you are, not for what you wear.*

*If people remember your*
*clothes you're overdressed.*

That's the way I was brought up.
That's the way I lived.

Then I met Rosalie, your favorite aunt.
She said she couldn't attend a wedding

although she wanted to.
Why? I asked.

*What's the point? I don't have a thing*
*to wear that will shock anyone.*

At the time, she was eighty, wore high heels
and narrow-legged silver lamé pants.

# Want

## Leslie Hodge

I'm a flaming drink
in the Tiki Bar, set
to catch your hair on fire.
I'll slip sugar in
the gas tank, bleed
the brake lines
of your sports car.

I'm dagger-eyes
and pouty lips,
strolling past you,
mouthing *asshole*.
I'm the bitch in six-
inch stilettos, stomping
on your heart.

I'm the ground glass
in your *foie gras*,
the mold on your *croissant*.
You think I do but, honest,
I got nothing that you want.
Yet when I call,
you will respond.

# Womxn

## Nikki Ashtiani

Show me what it's like to be a Womxn.
　　Show me the collection of every version of a Womxn,

who saw her fears and persisted through
　　blood, sweat, and tears to build *this* Womxn.

Regardless of skin tone or the ratio of hormones,
　　I see you, Womxn.

I know it's not easy to be a Womxn
　　in a world built by men, not tailored to a Womxn.

But remember,
　　you are not alone, Womxn.

Listen to the flock cheer,
　　we gather here for you, Womxn.

*This is a song, calling all Womxn,*

to step out of obedience,
　　may you be deviant, Womxn.

Were told your value lies
　　between your legs as a Womxn?

I see worth beyond the bed,
    show me the depth inside your head, Womxn.

Don't crumble at the hands of society,
    they want a *petite, polite, and pretty* Womxn,

a *patient, pleasant, perky* Womxn.
    Let their definitions be murky,

as we spell out,
    what it means to *be* a Womxn.

They may want a Barbie, but you are more than a toy,
    feel the power you employ, Womxn.


Build your empire on solid ground,
    let the vision of perfect drown before a child becomes a Womxn,

told they can only be one type of Womxn.
    Let them know a world built with respect for **any** Womxn.

It's time *we* show the world it is a blessing to be a Womxn.
    Paint me a new reality, show me what it's like to be a Womxn.

# La Promesa

## Jaquelin Fematt Dutson

La promesa
Prometo mi vida que nunca más
me ahogaré con la saliva de un tormento
porque la marea que yo llevo dentro
tan dentro de cada momento
es mi nombre que se desprende del silencio.

No quiero ofender mi vida
pero sé que en ti se esconde la herida
de esa palabra que traga y vomita
allá atrás
en la sed de otras semillas.

Hoy por eso prometo mi vida
que seguiré brotando de una vocal bonita
donde cae el verbo que pinta
a un paisaje
que yo no veía.

Esta promesa mía
no es sueño ni pesadilla
sino el nacer de una armonía
como el profundo respiro
de un ave sobre la brisa.

# Selfless Action

## Maryam Daftari

*You have control over action alone, never over its fruits. Live not for the fruits of action, nor attach yourself to inaction.*
—*Bhagavad Gita*, Chapter 2, Verse 47
Translated by Maharishi Mahesh Yogi

The hands that lift a burden unknown,
move with grace,
not bound by the fruits of action.

A cup of water in a stranger's palm,
offered with loving compassion,
not bound by the fruits of action.

A message of kindness whispered
inside the chaos of conflicts
not bound by the fruits of action.

A light in the dark, though no eyes may see still shines,
not bound by the fruits of action.

The tree gives shade to the weary below,
its roots faithful and deep,
not bound by the fruits of action.

Friendships that never fail to touch and heal
across unbounded obstacles
not bound by the fruits of action.

# Joshua Judges Ruth

## Bethel Swift

Jolene is a lioness.
Calculated. Cool. And coy.
She plays with my husband,
like a cat with its toy.

All they are to each other now,
another body to enjoy
pero no es importante
porque "a dondequiera que tú vayas,
iré yo" (o me voy).

En la guerra de los cuerpos
se acuerdan, ambos ganan.
Pero yo pago el precio
every single time.

En la madrugada, sexting satisfies.
Pero en la mañana, away from her phone,
la bella mujer con cara de bebe
mothers strong, sure, and alone—
never in need of a man to come home.

# Treacherous Beauty

## Jill G. Hall

I step outside front door
            in
                flip
                    flops

a tail teases me with the sound
of a shaman's    r  a  t  t  l  e.
Tined-tongue  flicks  furiously.

I want to retreat inside but puppy naps
on grass nearby. I'd been told this day
might come, hoped I'd have enough
courage to do what should be done.

Heart thumping, I slip into boots,
sneak out backdoor, straight,
for straight-edged shovel,
tiptoe across gravel,
raise tool above serpent's head.

      Dark
     diamonds
    shimmer in
     summer
      sun.

Unable to slay God's
creature I pause,
until he s l i t h e r s
under porch to haunt
me in my dreams.

# The Weight

## Meagan Marshall

We know the experience of being cornered—
things went too far, may have crossed the line,
tipped the scale, inspired denial.

A close call, what I name mine: the back of a truck,
shut camper shell. Six guys, strangers who offered
a ride, escape from the party busted by cops. Arrested
or deemed *arresting*—my choice.

My house just up the hill, makeup smeared, curfew broken,
just a small token of appreciation they wanted—
a kiss for each, no more, less than the price of gas,
not much to ask and I could keep
my skirt, my shirt intact.

Warm night air, my hair untouched. The key
slides noiselessly into its hole, the truck pulls out.
Then I Listerined the laugh from my lips, swallowed
the shame, the luck at having to give so little
when others have given, lost, been taken of much more—

Though this happened lines ago
like that Kunitz poem, I can feel my cheek still burning,
and nights seem sinister now. We know
when placed in the copper bowl, even small
assaults weigh.

# Mother's Day

## Courtney Anderson

I was young, freshly single, and desperately held onto several crumpled dollar bills.

Mother's Day was approaching, and my stomach churned thinking of what I couldn't afford.

I signed up for an oil on canvas class so I could create something money couldn't buy.

I painted a delicate row of purple pansies like the ones you tended to after each winter.

On Mother's Day, I nervously handed you my wrapped painting.

Your gaze stiffened as you undid the wrapping, revealing the purple brush strokes.

After a moment, you silently set down the painting.

Your finger tips with chipped, red nail polish grasped for a lighter and the end of a Marlboro Light began to burn.

You exhaled and the smoky air became as thick as the tension between us.

"You couldn't have treated your own mother to brunch?"

I looked at the painting.

The one thing I couldn't create was approval from you.

# Bar Code

## Susan E. Eyre

I found a barcode in the sand,
Striped pattern waiting to be scanned.
An unseen hand had deemed our worth
And stuck a label on the Earth,
As if the planet was for sale,
A bit of cosmos in retail.

What if a laser were to read
That code, to where would it then lead?
Would data stream to clerks above,
Who, reading ones and zeros of
The sticker sitting on the beach,
Would then some secret number reach?

I wondered what the price would show,
When valuations then did flow.
What number would the world be given?
Would figures stretch to lengths unbidden
Or would we be reduced to cost,
The value gone, the profits lost?

I leaned and grabbed the sticky tag
And walked it to a nearby bag
Of trash, which was where it belonged.
The answer'd come from far beyond:

No one could place a price upon
The Earth.
        There's no
                comparison.

# I Once Got Caught in a Fishing Net

## Thomas Courtney

I once became enmeshed in a fishing net, between
two wooden ships anchored at Songdo Beach,
on the eastern Sea of South Korea
desperate to catch any wave
and there, sand dollars lined the shore,
millions more than I'd ever seen back home,
though I guessed right that the trawlers
made waves off the jetty and I
found a piece of foam I thought would float as well as
my first thrift store board, that time I first fell in love with waves,
and also like the day I returned from Korea
and paddled past the California green foam, and the blinding
rain, which soaked the people lining the cliffs at Law Street,
the people who called the helicopter to save me from the waves
which the fishing nets in Pohang could not save me from
and from which I also do not want to be saved from
now that I am home in San Diego,
where sand dollars are rare,
but waves are plentiful.

# Way Over the Rainbow

## Joan Gerstein

In July we traveled the yellow brick road,
stifling heat, likes of which we've never known.
Lion, with no pride, sweat as we schlepped amid
shriveled apple orchards, parched poppy crops.
Scarecrow, not the sharpest scythe in the field,
feared spontaneous combustion. Oh, my!
Munchkins, clothes clinging on soggy skin, hid
as a rusty Tin Man creaked, his oil can empty.
Toto yelped to be toted as we trudged.
My feet were inflamed from ruby red slippers,
my dress, shredded limp from monkey claws.

Now, September, we reach the Imperial Palace
to meet the most popular, all-powerful wizard.
We enter through a back gate to find the place
a pig sty: fast food wrappers, torn up documents
strewn amidst piles of red hats and 23 boxes
of government files. The wiz appears in a smoke
screen with his lawyers, dismisses our requests.
He has Tin Man removed due to his silver skin
and kicks out Lion, saying that there's only room
for one king in this jungle. "You're dumb as dirt
but loyal," he tells Scarecrow, "You can be
my sentry." He gives me his million dollar smile,
"Return tonight after you get rid of these losers.
You can sign an NDA and be my apprentice."

# Vowels Softening to Liquid in My Mouth

## Janine Canillas

My tongue is as dry as the Sahara,
It's as sticky as a dog licking for a treat.
At 130 degrees, Canada is burning,
New Orleans and Venice are underwater

I want to swear at the corporations
And politicians who put their money on—
Right leg first. I'll put 20 down for water.
One day, it will all be controlled by Nestle,
And I will have to pay to swim in the ocean
For any sense of relief.

Rather than soften my vowels and speak sweet,
I will turn my lines into poetry,
And my hump on my back from working
18-hour days in front of the computer
Will grow into that of a shark fin,
Curved and jagged from bending over.

People will come and snap a selfie.
It will trend on social—
The screaming, cursing human-shark

That once saw Atlantis and sipped on fresh water
Free of chlorine, bubbling with children's laughter.

# In the Killing Fields of Cheung Ek

### Janice Alper

In monsoon season bones
surface from shallow graves.
A ring is washed up—is it
from the hand of a mother,
a wife, a grandparent?—sniff
the damp air, and find other
remnants of past lives hidden
among the soggy leaves.

The nearby Buddhist Memorial
houses the displaced bones. In a
whisper, I recite a Jewish prayer
for the departed.

Back in Phnom Penh children
run up to me, stand on tiptoes
to touch my white hair—a rarity
among them—giggle. They call
me *Yi-ey*, Grandma. I laugh and
smile, hug them. We are alive,
*no victory for a mad man here.*

# US Sway

## Carol Shamon

You fooled us
In those duck and cover days
I believed your pledge
but really?
Under god?
Under our desks
Buying it all
buying EVERYTHING
The dream offered
houses for all
except behind the red line
Our TV's changed
from black and white
to living color
but forgot to show us
true indigenous red
the real story of black
browns it turned out
were not lazy
Your dirty Chinese laundry
is showing
All the underwear lined up
pink for girls
and blue for boys
but what about that luminous spectrum
arching over the clothesline?

\*\*\*

We saved our money
our little dimes marched
The less we had
the more you took
We wanted backyard bar-b-que
but paid for bombs
Amazons took over
As we plodded like zombies
holding our little computers
fused to our eyes
trying to calculate
the heat
that's burning
us alive

# Why Do Black Lives Matter?

## Tomás Gayton

When every day we see them lost by legal lynching
Easy targets for the police and the press
to stigmatize and demonize
because of our color
Why must we relive America's bloody history
of slavery, Black Codes and Jim Crow
with daily accounts of legal lynching?
Why in this new century do
Black Deaths Matter?

# Fentanyl Fugue

## Aryeh Cantos

You go to sleep
And then you're gone

Your head propped
on a cobblestone
the obelisk of almost lived
Hair shorn
tracked vein
spirit almost born

You go to sleep
and then you're gone

From this room
this cell
this home
this hell

This almost lover
left to almost mourn

What is accident?
And what intent?
The reaper comes
and wants the rent

But first the needle
and the heated spoon
You almost promised her
You'd come back soon

Now watch this almost lover
Almost break
Now see
this streak of tears
on her face
your head on the
pillow of her hand

What is this nursery rhyme
that no one sees
eluding passersby
adrift in time
An alley
An ashtray
A cardboard box
the almost things you left behind
and she the only witness to your sleep

# Cradleboard

## Carol Moscrip

They let her sink into death
before their very eyes, her parents;
the court order for the transfusion
came too late. Her fifteen-year-old
boyfriend's family will raise the baby,
and the young mother
can proceed to heaven's gates,
her gaunt face, pale blue
from the draining;
Christ cares about the count
of our blood in drops,
her parents believe
and rejoice that their daughter
died pure of body untainted
by a stranger's fluid in her veins.
The Navajo grandmother swaddles
the baby, puts a fingertip on his lips
until the nurse brings the first bottle.
The cradleboard is waiting.

# Ode to Tyranny

## Ali Arsanjani

O Tyranny, thou subtle hand,
That moves before the law's command.
In shadows first, your whispers creep,
Obey in silence, bend, or weep.
No need for force, when fear abides—
When trust in rule of law subsides.

Your path is paved by hands that yield,
To one bright banner on the field.
With every choice, each vote erased,
Beware the one-party state embraced.
And when the facts are spun as lies,
You grin, for truth in darkness dies.

Paramilitaries rise to cheer,
To stoke the fires of rampant fear.
When words are sharp and ethics fall,
You dance through broken halls of law.
No institution dares to stand,
As you extend your iron hand.

Yet still we see, in silent night,
The courage needed for this fight.
O Tyranny, you thrive in dread,
But we will not bow low our head.

For truth persists, through storm and sin,
And kindness shall yet rise, and win.

# Elegy for Denis, with Dogs

## Patricia Aya Williams

After retirement, you loved to walk in the woods.

> *The dogs know me now. They know*
> *I've got something for them.*

Every day—coat pulled close
biscuits in pockets—you walked in the woods

until you couldn't
walk anymore.

Did the dogs        wonder
where you went?

You are still   w a l k i n g   t h r o u g h   w o o d s
From a            distance

dogs catch
your scent       tug their leads— —    —         —    —

Some  begin  to  bark … …

...break
   ing

      free

     theygorunning
      to greet you

# Glints of Gold

## Al Brown

Time has a way of collapsing
when you least expect it,
folding
       like a map,
bringing distant moments
unexpectedly together.

This morning on the beach,
dogs thrashing the water,
the sun sparked glints of gold
     in the sand—while

            six
          thousand
       miles
     and seventeen years ago
the sun sparked glints of gold
     on a beach
where I walked with another—
     without dogs,
       without love,
         without hope.

Holding both moments was
     jarring.
I am not now who I was then.

I would not change what happened
in that other place.
I only wish
            the other me
        could have read the promise
in that glinting sand—

could have known
that dogs and love come
                        and go
but there is always
        hope.

# The Linda Vista Community Garden

### Steve Rodriguez

As election time nears,
the seeds recently planted
will soon bear fall fruit.
A San Diego working class neighborhood
finds new citizens casting ballots
for the first time.
Roots now entrenched
in this soil, nurtured by
California water and sun,
education and observation,
signal an investment in
the community's well-being.
Expected to produce dividends sprouting
in the form of civic engagement.

And so it is within
the planter beds of this new garden.
Seeds sowed on a spring day
have now grown stalks and stems.
Ripening peppers, squash, corn—
reaching far above the surface.
Subjects of pride and admiration.
A diverse mixture of generational

knowledge and experience
transplanted from the Sonoran desert,
the Guatemalan highlands,
Vietnamese deltas,
and just down the block,
is combined with a coastal clime
to produce a yield for the dinner table,
as well as encourage a firmer grip on this land.

# Song of the Faith-Bird

## Jim Moreno

*Faith is the bird that feels the light when the dawn is still dark*
—Rabindranath Tagore

When the darkness around us is deep
my faith-bird flies to my soul-house.

The light from my faith-bird fills my
soul-house with the light of essentials,

the light of dawn, the light of kindness,
the light of that which navigates
the unknown curve.

My soul-house is always a place of safety,
a place of creativity, a place where the glass is
always, every time, half full.

In times when I'm feeling like I'm drowning,
a light from my soul-house buoys me up.

You see I've been in terrible storms at sea—
ocean in all directions to the horizon,
towering waves three stories high,
crashing down on my ship, all of us,
even the captain, miserably seasick.

In that endless storm my faith-bird perched
on my shoulder whispering strengths in my ear:

I fly to you in peace, I fly to you in mystery,
I fly to you in kindness, Because of me
faith is something you feel,
not an essential of your mind.

This storm will end. All storms will end.
Remember after every storm you'll find ways to be useful.

Utility is stored in safety in your soul-house,
waiting for you to use in many ways so you'll never be alone.
For that reason we must always embrace mystery,
We must always risk delight.

# About the Authors

**Adhara Mereles** was born in Mexico and raised in California. She earned a bachelor's degree from the University of San Francisco and a master's degree from Columbia University. Her work appears in the anthology, *A Year in Ink, Volume 17*, in the online journal *Red Rose Thorns*, in San Diego City Works Press' anthology, *Sunshine/Noir III*, and in the *San Diego Poetry Annual* 2024–25. Beyond prose and poetry, Adhara enjoys photography, playing the piano, and discovering life alongside loved ones.

**Aimee Truchan** is a (mostly) fiction writer who moonlights as a healthcare marketing executive. She is also an instructor at San Diego Writers, Ink. Her work has been published in *A Year in Ink, Volumes 13-15*, *The Decameron Project*, Roi Fainéant Literary Press, and Dimestories.org.

**Al Brown:** This one is for Teya.

**Alejandra Navarro** is a writer and marketing and communications consultant based in Carlsbad, California. She holds degrees from University of California San Diego, Quinnipiac University, and Columbia University's Graduate School of Journalism. Alejandra began her career as a journalist before moving into strategic communications for universities, foundations, and marketing agencies. She is currently at work on a novel that traces the lives of three generations of Latina women in California, exploring the sacrifices they make to keep a long-buried family tragedy from surfacing.

**Dr. Ali Arsanjani** is a Rumi scholar and has been translating and providing commentary on the poetry of the renowned mystical poet Jalaledin Rumi for the past thirty-five years. He is the author of *A Wave in the Ocean: Commentary and Analysis of the Poetry of Rumi* (1998) and is completing a book entitled *Rumi's Guide for Lovers and Spiritual Seekers*. His poetry has been published in *Lyrical Iowa* and *A Step In Between*, as well as in the *A Year in Ink* anthology and *San Diego Poetry Annual*. His recent book is a translation and commentary, in English ghazal form, of the ghazals of the renowned Persian poet Hafez of Shiraz, entitled *The Words That Bring Us to Dance* (2024). In his non-poetry profile, Ali is an adjunct professor of computer science in artificial intelligence and machine learning at University of California San Diego and San Jose State University. He is also a director of applied AI engineering at Google.

**Amy Strommer** is a writer, teacher, mother, runner, and avid reader who is always five minutes late. She lives in San Diego with her family and wonderful dog, Kelly. Amy enjoys writing about motherhood, life, and whatever other topics enter her brain at 3 a.m. as she is staring at the ceiling willing her body to go to sleep. Though humor is her love language, sometimes a serious piece will land on the page. She is in the editing stages of a memoir about the ten years her family lived in wine country, *California: What Doesn't Kill You Makes Your Anxieties Stronger*. She is also working on a romance novel, *For a Moment in France*. Find her obsessively searching for books to add to her Want to Read list in her GoodReads app.

**Anne Randerson, PhD**, has taught creative writing courses since 2007 and teaches online workshops for San Diego Writers, Ink. As a creative writing coach and developmental editor, Anne helps global writers unleash their creative expressions. In addition to publishing short stories, poems, and essays in international publications, Anne has released two novels under a pseudonym. She is a member of the San Diego Writers and Editors Guild, Golden Crown Literary Society, Belgian Audiovisual Screenwriters Association, and SABAM (Belgian Association of Authors, Composers, and Publishers). To contact Anne, visit www.crossculturalhorizons.com.

**Aryeh Cantos** uses simple language to make unusual observations in a compassionate way. When not working to pay the bills or writing (which doesn't pay the bills but seems more important), he practices Aikido, the way of harmony, somewhere in San Diego.

**Barbara Bowley** is an anthropologist whose research focuses on relationships, intimacy, and aging through her work at pauseprofessors. com. Barbara is a former university library director, pioneer in information literacy education, champion horse racing handicapper, open-minded skeptic, and enthusiastic student of almost any topic. Born in New York and a San Diegan by choice, she's convinced San Diego is, in fact, America's Finest City.

**Bernie Nofel** has been an active member of San Diego's writing community since Old Towne was just called "Town." He has published a psychodrama mystery, *Mirror Mirror: A Mystery*, and is honored to have had previous pieces accepted in *A Year in Ink* anthologies. He's a dreamer and a believer in dreams, even though his writing is prone to evoking nightmares in readers. :)

**Bethel Swift** is a San Diego-based mixed media artist and poet. She is the author/publisher of *Conversations with Good Men*. For more information, please visit www.bethelswift.com.

**Carol Moscrip**, author of poetry and Dime Stories, has written six chapbooks and a book of poems, *Straw*, and has a manuscript ready for publication, *Escape Artist*. She has most recently published in *A Year in Ink* and *San Diego Poetry Annual* and is a Pushcart nominee.

**Carol Shamon** is a writer and painter living in San Diego. Her first collection of poetry, *Stronger Than Salmon* (Finishing Line Press), was published in September 2024. Her second collection, *Art Type: Boats Against the Current*, comes out in June 2025. Other recent publications appear in *Seedlings, Summation, Relevant Poetry, Spillwords, RedRoseThorns*, and the *San Diego Poetry Annual*. She was an Honorable Mention in the 2023 Ocean-Earth-Air Art and Poetry book and in 2024 for the 10th Annual Memoir Showcase. In 2020 Irrelevant Press published her 'zine *A Different More: Creating and Embracing Change*

*While Aging.* The 'zine *Oh The Water* was published in the summer of 2023. She is currently working on her memoir *The Decade House.*

**Cherie Kephart** is a developmental editor, writing coach, and award-winning author of the inspirational memoir, *A Few Minor Adjustments.* She is a two-time winner of the San Diego Memoir Showcase, has been published in more than twenty anthologies, and is a workshop facilitator at several writing conferences and retreats.

**Claire Hsu Accomando** was born in Switzerland to a French-Armenian mother and a Chinese father. She spent her early childhood in France during World War II. Her memoir *Love and Rutabaga* (St. Martin's Press) was recently released in French and is due to be re-issued later this year by The Press at Cal Poly Humboldt. Accomando graduated from New York University with a science degree but was always drawn more to the arts. Her poetic memoir *Evaporation* was published by The Press at Cal Poly Humboldt in 2025. *Lifting Elephants* is forthcoming from Third Coast Press. Accomando's poems have also appeared in journals including *Atlanta Review, Mudfish, Toyon, Bullets into Bells,* and several anthologies. She lives in Bonita, California, and defines poetry as distillation: You start out with a truckload of potatoes and end up with a shot of vodka.

**Courtney Anderson**, a writer published in *A Celebration of Young Poets Minnesota and Wisconsin* (Fall 2001), lives in San Diego with her husband, Mike, and their mini-goldendoodle, Leo. Born and raised in Wisconsin, her love for poetry started at an early age. She enjoys exploring the California coastline and diving into memoirs and coming-of-age fiction.

**Donna Jones** is working hard on her first historical novel about Countess Adele, daughter of William the Conqueror.

**Jamey Annette Fitzpatrick** is a recent graduate in speech-language pathology and has made her living working with spoken and written language. She's written poetry, plays, and short stories since she was a teenager. Writing has kept her afloat and sane in this crazy world. Her poems and short stories have been published in *A Year in Ink,*

*Cellar Roots*, *Bard's West*, *Dawn Horizons*, and the *San Diego Poetry Annual*, and her plays were featured in symposiums at Eastern Michigan University. She was grateful to be awarded grants to lead a student research team providing clinical support to students with Long Covid at California State University, Northridge.

**Janet Travers** has written a collection of forty short stories. She has been published in the 2023 edition of *The Guilded Pen* and the soon-to-be-released 2025 edition. She won a short story contest hosted by *Tulip Tree Review* Humor Edition #14, 2023. She was one of the top ten finalists for the 2024 8th Annual Matchbook Story Contest hosted by the San Diego Library Foundation. Currently, she is halfway through a novel about a complicated, annoying woman whom we like to dislike. She has written and performed original songs and a stage play. For Janet, writing is not an escape from reality but a way to understand and figure out people and life experiences. She is a singer who started performing professionally at age sixteen. She graduated from San Diego State University with a theater degree and has enjoyed performing for stage, film, and TV in New York and California. She is honored to have a story included in *A Year in Ink, Volume 18*.

**Janice Alper**, an active octogenarian, writes poems, personal essays, and memoirs. She attributes her growth as a writer in the late stage of her life to San Diego Writers, Ink and to the specific guidance of Judy Reeves and Jim Moreno. Janice's memoir, *Sitting on the Stoop: A Girl Grows in Brooklyn, 1944–1957*, is available on Amazon. She is currently enrolled in the Creative Writing Program—Poetry at San Diego State University. You can follow her at www.janicesjottings1.com.

**Janine Canillas** is a TV and video game writer whose work spans poetry, journalism, and children's literature. Her writing has appeared in publications such as *The Guardian* and *Business Insider*. Her poetry has been featured in *Broad Sound*, *Slow Lightning*, and here in *A Year in Ink*. She's also the author of the children's book *Lenny Peed on That!*

**Jaquelin Fematt Dutson** is a poet and one of the contributing authors of the award-winning book *Déjame que te cuente*. She presents at conferences and book festivals and is engaged in a wide range of collaborations.

**Jill G. Hall** is author of the Anne McFarland Series. Her poems have been published in a variety of anthologies. Her next book, *On a Sundown Sea: A Novel of Madame Tingley and the Origins of Lomaland*, will be released in October 2025. www.jillghall.com

**Jim Moreno** is a poetry-teaching artist with San Diego Writers, Ink. His free online poetry class for veterans is called "How We Say It: Pens Moving Across the Page."

**Joan Gerstein**, a retired educator and psychotherapist, is beginning her eighth year of teaching creative writing to incarcerated veterans. Joan has been penning poetry since elementary school, and her first book of poetry, *Theories of Relativity*, was published in 2021 by Garden Oak Press.

**Leslie Hodge** lives in San Diego. Her poems appear in *Catamaran Literary Reader*, *The Main Street Rag*, *South Florida Poetry Journal*, *ONE ART*, *Whale Road Review*, *Sheila-Na-Gig*, and elsewhere. Her debut chapbook, *Escape and Other Poems*, was published by Kelsay Books in 2024. Currently she is reading for *The Adroit Journal*. Visit her at www.lesliehodgepoet.com.

**Lucy Lehman** is a poet and author of fiction, living in San Diego.

A graduate of the University of Michigan, **M. Annette Ketner**'s poetry and prose have been published in several anthologies including *A Year in Ink*, *Shaking the Tree*, *San Diego Poetry Anthology*, and *Bards Across the Pond*, as well as *Memoir Showcase*. Her greatest joy is seeing her daughter's poems and short stories also published.

**Maria Zaragoza** is a writer born and raised in San Diego. She is receiving her bachelor's degree in English and Comparative Literature from San Diego State University. She writes historical fiction and magical realism and is a lover of all media and coffee.

**Marie Lagos** writes books for young and new adults—and for adults like her, who wonder if they'll ever feel like grown-ups. When she's not making up stories, she's an attorney, a mom to two, a wife to one, and an unpaid chauffeur, cook, and laundress to many.

**Maryam Daftari** is a retired lecturer in political science and a China specialist. She is a poet, pianist, and award-winning nature photographer. Maryam has published three books and over twenty-five articles on Chinese affairs, and has lectured on international relations and comparative politics, specifically on Chinese government and politics, at several universities for over three decades. She started writing poetry as an undergraduate, winning several awards. Maryam's poems have been chosen for publication in many of the annual editions of *Lyrical Iowa* and *San Diego Poetry Annual* (2013–2024), *A Year in Ink* (2023), and *Stand Forth* and *A Step Between*, publications of Iowa's Society of Great River Poets. Her poems have also appeared in an anthology of San Diego poets entitled *Sundays at Liberty Station*. She has won first place in Traditional Poetry Style in a competition by the Iowa Poetry Association in 2024 for "By One Degree." Maryam is the author of three poetry collections: *Like Magic but Real, Haiku Workbook*, and *Kintsugi: Poems of Hope and Healing*. Her favorite poets are Rumi and Mary Oliver.

**Meagan Marshall** is a poet, performer, and professor. Her work has appeared in various journals, including *The Portland Review, Web Del Sol, San Diego Poetry Annual, Charlotte: A Journal of Literature, Sunshine/Noir III, A Year in Ink*, and elsewhere. She has been commissioned by San Diego Dance Theater to write and perform several micro-fictions with the company. She teaches in the Department of English and Comparative Literature at San Diego State University, where she is a recipient of the Pitt and Virginia Warner Innovation Award and Director of the Hugh C. Hyde Living Writers Series. She is also managing editor of *Poetry International*.

**Michelle Goering**, a writer and musician with a background in publishing, is passionate about the power of words to connect and transform. A Baha'i and city dweller of four decades, she grew up in a Mennonite community on a Kansas farm.

**Nikki Ashtiani** is a writer based in San Diego with an interest in exploring themes of womanhood, nature, and creativity in her work.

**Patricia Aya Williams** is a Red Wheelbarrow Poetry Prize recipient and Steve Kowit Poetry Prize finalist. She lives with her husband, Chris, and dog, Binxy, in San Diego. More of her work can be found at www.beingpatricia.com.

**Saadia Ali Esmail** is working on her first memoir about arranged marriages and her experience as a Pakistani-American. She has three children ranging in age from twelve to nineteen who love to keep her on her toes. Her pieces have been included in *Shaking the Tree, Volumes 2, 5, and 6*. She has also been published in *A Year in Ink, Volumes 13, 16, and 17*. She volunteers on the Board of the International Memoir Writers Association as treasurer and looks forward to working with the talented writing community in San Diego.

**Steve Rodriguez** is a retired U.S. Marine Corps officer and a retired high school English teacher. He is co-editor of *The Linda Vista Update* digital newsletter.

**Susan E. Eyre** grew up in Istanbul, Turkey, and now writes from her home in San Diego. Her poetry is about the beauty, the magic, and especially the humor she sees in the world around her. "Bar Code" is Susan's first published poem.

In her quest to become the world's greatest mother, **Tammy Tollner** forgot all about her love for writing until she quit pinot grigio, a social crutch that worked for years before a painful divorce and worldwide pandemic sent her Wine Mom status into overdrive. A former book-and-beer-loving journalism major and daughter of the head football coach at University of Southern California, Tammy wrote commercials at a Los Angeles advertising agency before quitting work to stay home and raise her three daughters, now thirty-one, twenty-nine, and twenty-six. A seventh-generation native Californian, Tammy eventually married again and added three sons, twenty-nine, twenty-seven, and twenty, into the mix. She's currently writing a memoir recounting the roller coaster path and astonishing life transformations that have occurred since quitting booze in her fifties. She has plans for a second book that will chronicle the tales of her early California ancestors who arrived in San Diego from New Spain in 1769, bearing only the clothes on their backs and a few precious cuttings of grapevine.

**Thomas Courtney** is a middle school teacher in southeast San Diego. In 2021, Thomas was selected as the San Diego Unified School District Teacher of the Year. He writes for many educational periodicals and has published several books, including *Stabone, What Melancholy Used to Be*, and the fantasy series Law Firms and Librarians under the pen name T. Oliver Courtney. When not teaching or writing, Thomas is usually riding his cafe racer motorcycles, surfing, or growing the best Early Girl tomatoes in San Diego.

**Tomás Gayton** was born and raised in Seattle, Washington, the grandson of African American pioneers. Tomás is a retired civil rights attorney/activist. He co-founded San Diego Poet's Press and taught many verse writing/poetry classes, including at the University of California San Diego Craft Center. He is a world traveler who lives in San Diego. His poetry is his life in verse.

**Victoria Derr Valencia** is a writer whose work focuses on the self, devotion, love, healing, fear, and the holy act of returning to oneself.

# About the Editors

**Vera Sanchez** is a native of San Diego and grew up in Logan Heights. She is a published author of two novels, *Prison Letters: Walking to Honor* and *Puto*. Her debut children's book, *Jada's Dance for Chicano Park*, was voted the Best Children's Book by the San Diego Book Awards Association and was a semi-finalist in the national book competition Winning Writers. She has also been a writing judge for the NAACP San Diego High School Chapter and the San Diego City College Scholarship Committee. She received her B.A. in English, California Teaching Credential in English, and M.A. in Education from San Diego State University. She has been an English teacher for over twenty years. Many of her students have won county and statewide writing competitions in addition to having their work published. Vera is currently a full-time professor at San Diego Mesa College.

**W.A. Fulkerson** is a novelist (*For Whom the Sun Sings, The Weathermen, the Starfall Trilogy*), an award-winning screenwriter (*Save My Seoul*), and a prolific ghostwriter. Born and raised in San Diego, California, he has been a regular instructor at San Diego Writers, Ink since 2016. Today, he lives in Georgia with his wife and three children but continues to teach virtual (and occasionally in-person) classes at San Diego Writers, Ink. W.A. Fulkerson's work is influenced by his lifelong love of wrestling, Brazilian jiujitsu, the Romantic poets, high mythology, and grappling with big questions.

# About San Diego Writers, Ink

San Diego Writers, Ink is a nonprofit literary arts organization dedicated to nurturing writers and celebrating the written word. Through classes, workshops, readings, community events, and publishing opportunities, we support writers of all backgrounds and levels. Rooted in creativity, connection, and craft, we serve as a vibrant hub for San Diego's literary community.

Everyone has a story. Write yours right now.

www.writeyourstorynow.org